A HAPPY CHRISTMAS CEILIDH

(THE SHROUDED ISLE SERIES)

ZOE TASIA

Huntsville, Texas, USA

Also by Zoe Tasia

The Shrouded Isle
Kilts and Catnip
Bagpipes and Basil
A Happy Christmas Ceilidh

Watch for more at zoetasia.com.

Table of Contents

GENRE: FANTASY/PARANORMAL/SHIFTERS 1

Chapter 1 | Becca 2

Chapter 2 | Becca 12

Chapter 3 | Tate 15

Chapter 4 | Greg 22

Chapter 5 | Jessie 26

Chapter 6 | Becca 38

Chapter 7 | Tate 42

Chapter 8 | Jessie 44

Chapter 9 | Greg 49

Chapter 10 | Becca 54

Chapter 11 | Becca 62

The End 66

Continue reading for a sneak peek of books 1 and 2 of the series............. 67

KILTS AND CATNIP | Shrouded Isle, Scotland 69

BAGPIPES AND BASIL | Shrouded Isle, Scotland 78

Spring Shenanigans | The Shrouded Isle | Zoe Tasia 96

SPRING SHENANIGANS 98

GENRE: FANTASY/PARANORMAL/ SHIFTERS

A HAPPY CHRISTMAS CEILIDH

Copyright © 2022 by Zoe Tasia

Cover Design GetCovers

All cover art copyright © 2022

All Rights Reserved

This edition published by Zoe Tasia (Huntsville, Texas, USA) in 2022

Library of Congress Control Number:

PRINT ISBN: 978-1-7350689-6-1[1]

EBOOK ISBN: 978-1-7350689-5-4[2]

Publisher's Cataloging-in-Publication data

Names: Tasia, Zoe, author.

Title: A Happy Christmas Ceilidh / Zoe Tasia.

Series: The Shrouded Isle

Description: Huntsville, TX: Zoe Tasia, 2023.

Identifiers: LCCN: 2023903964 | ISBN: 978-1-7350689-6-1 (print) | 978-1-7350689-5-4 (ebook)

Subjects: LCSH Islands—Scotland—Fiction. | Americans—Scotland—Fiction. | Man-woman relationships—Fiction. | Family—Fiction. | Fairies—Scotland—Fiction. | Shapeshifters—Fiction. | Magic—Fiction. | Christmas—Fiction. | Scotland—Fiction. | Romance fiction. | Fantasy fiction. | BISAC FICTION / Fantasy / Romance | FICTION / Fairy Tales, Folk Tales, Legends & Mythology | FICTION / Romance / Clean & Wholesome | FICTION / Romance / Fantasy | FICTION / Romance / Paranormal / Shifters | FICTION / Holidays

Classification: LCC PS3620 .A82 H37 2023 | DDC 813.6—dc23

---

1. https://www.myidentifiers.com/title_registration?isbn=978-1-7350689-6-1&icon_type=Assigned

2. https://www.myidentifiers.com/title_registration?isbn=978-1-7350689-5-4&icon_type=Assigned

Chapter 1
Becca

I'd just passed the basket of dinner rolls to Greg, my boyfriend, when he froze and his eyes widened. "Rebecca, don't move," he whispered. "There's a wee man leering at you."

"What man?" I asked.

Greg shook his head. "Dinna spook him. He's nae a pixie, and I dinna sense he's fae. I'm not sure what he is. Maybe a witch made a wee manikin to torment us."

I had a pretty good idea what he saw. On a whim, I illuminated the room with my collection of Christmas-themed glass tea lights. Though we could see each other clearly, the low light distorted items in the distance. From my daughters' expressions, they knew what he saw, but instead of explaining it, they surprised me.

My fifteen-year-old daughter whipped her head around and gasped. "I see it too," Jessie whispered. "Do you think it's poisonous?"

Tate, my youngest, shivered in mock fear. "I hope not. Mr. Greg may be allergic."

"The nasty peeping tom willna get a chance." In one fluid motion, Greg stood and hurled a dinner roll at Sir Clifford, our elf on the shelf. He nailed the toy hard, driving it to the back of the counter.

Greg grabbed his napkin and sprinted over. He reached, then howled, jerking his hand back. "The wee bugger bit me!" He displayed a bleeding finger.

By now, the girls couldn't contain themselves. "Shame on you, Sir Clifford!" Jessie said between giggles.

Tate shook her finger in the doll's direction. "You're a bad elf. We're going to report *you* to Santa."

The girls howled with laughter and ran to the counter.

"Dinna touch it!" Greg warned. "The nasty thing may have germs."

"It's okay, Greg. We'll protect you from Sir Clifford," Jessie said. She reached in carefully, mindful not to cut herself on whatever Greg had, tugged out the doll and showed it to him.

"Uh oh," Tate said. "You're both in trouble. No touching the elf!"

Jessie held her stomach and laughed. Between her guffaws, she said, "The big strong Keeper and banisher of fae—tricked by a doll!"

"Let me see him." I examined Sir Clifford and found a place on his leg where a wire had sawed through the cloth. Years ago, I'd wired the elf to make him more poseable, and Greg must have snatched it hard enough to scrape his finger on the sharp edge.

When the girls were little, I'd heard mothers mention the Elf on the Shelf at toddler group and even seen photos. But I knew nothing about it other than they looked the same as the elves my mother arranged on a white ladder by the Christmas tree every year. Those elves made the trip to Florida with my parents when they retired, and I was in no hurry to inherit them. They always gave me the creeps, as did the shelf elves. When Jessie was five, she asked me why we didn't have one and I doubted my explanation that the dolls freaked Mommy out would cut it. Jess chose a first name for him and Tate gave him a middle name. The queen knighted our elf at some point, so his full name is Sir Clifford Elvin Fields-Shaw. Clifford, for *Clifford, the Big Red Dog*. And Elvin, because he's an elf. He got two last names since I kept my maiden name and the girls didn't want daddy to feel left out. My late husband and I had agreed the girls in the family would get my last name and the boys his. Truth be told, I found Sir Clifford to be pretty shudder-inducing too, but at least he had a name, and somehow, that made it better. Then again, Chucky had a name, and he turned out to be a psychopath-killer doll.

Greg eyed Sir Clifford. "Why is that thing in your kitchen?"

"It's a tradition. A fairly modern one that I only found out about after I had kids."

"Aye."

"*The Elf on the Shelf: A Family Tradition* is a book by Carol Aebersold and her daughter Chandra Bell. In the story, St. Nicholas has friends called "scout elves." These elves spy on families and return to the North Pole each night to report on the inhabitants' behaviors."

"Didna sound like any I'd want nearby. Wee clipes."

I shrugged. "They help Santa with the naughty and nice lists. Each morning, the elf returns to a new location in the home and the children must find him. The elves become magical by being loved and named by their family.

The book comes with a box containing an elf to name, and—voila—you had your very own elf on a shelf. The elf sticks around until Christmas Eve. Then it's time for elf vacay with Malibu Barbie until next year."

"Who's Malibu Barbie? She isna coming too, is she?"

Hoping to stifle a case of the giggles, I pressed a fist against my mouth as I shook my head.

The last day of November, I took the elf from its box and smoothed his coat. It was late and I wanted to find a place to hide him that would give the girls a bit more of a challenge, but be inaccessible to our kitten.

I put the elf behind a cookie jar I rarely filled because of my horrific attempts at baking. The girls discovered the hiding place in less than a minute. I'd forgotten all about him by the time Greg arrived for dinner, and it hadn't occurred to me my dear Scot wouldn't know about the custom.

To deter the girls from touching the elf, I added the rule that anyone who handled him had to sing a song to Sir Clifford, but whoever resisted the temptation would get to choose the song. By this time, we had an entire repertoire of obnoxious, goofy holiday songs. I kept the handmade songbook and kazoo on the desk and let Tate look through it.

"Why would anyone want a creepy stuffed doll spying on you?" he asked, eyeing the elf with distaste.

"I gotta say, I don't like stuffed elves either, but it's all in the name of fun and now that you're in on it, you can help me find places to hide him."

"Aye." Greg grinned. Something told me tomorrow morning the girls would wake up to find the elf in a very entertaining locale. Hopefully, Greg would do what I hadn't by wowing them with his ingenuity.

Knowing her sister well, Tate chose the song, "I Want a Hippopotamus for Christmas." As Jessie sang and Tate played the kazoo, Greg whispered what his intricate plan was. "And I'm coming for breakfast," he announced with a flourish.

I smiled. "Wanting to see how the girls react, I gather. You know what they say about the curious cat. You might get more than you bargained for."

"Mmph, I'm a seasoned Keeper. I can handle anything."

As Keeper of the Forest, Greg could detect fae and return any escaped ones back to their home in the forest. After falling in love with the handsome Scot, I remained on the island to help him with his Keeper duties.

"Anything, huh. Even two teenage girls?" I asked.

Greg snorted. "Tis a challenge, but I'm ready. Have your phone with the wee camera out for photos," Greg suggested.

Greg stayed until the girls went to sleep. Afterwards, we worked on Operation Hidden Elf.

I wondered if it would even occur to the girls to blame Greg for the prank. They thought him overly serious. When he encountered something unfamiliar, he became stoic, which the girls thought was hilarious. In his defense, he'd not experienced current culture first hand in hundreds of years. Considering the losses he'd sustained in his life and his Keeper duty to protect people from the fae, I could understand. It was always nice to see him in a playful mood, but usually I'm the only one he shows that side to. When I said goodnight to the girls, I'd told them that Greg was coming for breakfast, so it wouldn't surprise them when they woke and found him at the table.

Between the two of us, we set up the prank.

Before he left, Greg and I had a glass of whisky.

"It's nice playing a trick on someone else for a change," Greg noted, as he stifled a yawn.

I poked his flat stomach. "Who's been playing tricks on you?"

"It's been a while, but a group pranked me but good in my earliest days as Keeper."

Remembering how he felt about a certain fae, I made a guess. "It must be pixie-related."

"Aye, and that's all you'll get from me aboot it."

"Meanie!" I teased.

Greg sighed and stood. "I'll tell ye someday after we're married, and it's too late to ditch me for being a gowk." His accent broadened as he grew tired and his low voice rumbled pleasantly.

I took his calloused hand, as we walked to the door and paused, unwilling to part. "A gowk? Will you at least tell me what that is?" I asked, tilting my head back to gaze into his green eyes. He always smelled of the forest—my cheeks suffused with warmth at the scent of frost-kissed leaves, crisp pine needles, and loam, sleeping under a blanket of snow.

He tugged me close as he answered. "A fool."

"Never," I breathed as his lips met mine.

#

The next morning, I'd barely washed my face and slipped on a robe when I heard tapping on my bedroom window. It was still dark outside, but Greg stood with his nose pressed to the glass. When he saw me, he placed a finger across his lips and motioned toward the front door.

I tiptoed out and let him in.

"Have they been up?" he whispered.

"If they have, they didn't turn on the lights and it's too dark to see anything."

Greg gleefully rubbed his hands together. His eyes gleamed.

"You're having a lot of fun with this, aren't you?"

"Aye."

I put the kettle on for tea.

"How long are they going to sleep?" Greg asked.

"Listen for the kettle while I get ready. I need to be out of the bathroom before they wake or we'll be fighting over the sink. Now that I have a tween and a teen, it's a constant battle for the mirror."

When I came back, he had found scones and fruit and put them out for breakfast. "Sit. Water's ready. I'll make you a cuppa."

When I heard Jessie yell, "Shame on you, Sir Cliff!" I knew the girls were awake.

The girls murmured to each other, and a minute later, they joined us.

"Sir Cliff stole my new art pencils!" Tate complained.

"*You* can buy more pencils," Jessie said. "He stole the necklace Gavin got me!"

At the carnival, Jessie's boyfriend, Gavin Samms, won a necklace with a red ceramic heart for her. Though of sentimental value for Jess, Gavin probably spent ten times what the necklace was worth. Even now, the chain was oxidizing.

Greg and I played dumb. "What's happened?" I asked.

"Are the fae playing pranks on ye?" Greg said a moment later.

"Come on," Tate said, tugging me up from my chair.

We'd dressed Sir Cliff in a black cape made from a trash bag liner and taped a toothpick wand to his hand. He rode a broom made from one of our old paint brushes. I also reinforced the seams, so he no longer had wire poking out. Greg fashioned a pair of black, wire-framed glasses from pipe cleaners he found in the shed. Sir Clifford hovered above the girls' beds. Greg had strung nylon thread between the two small ceiling lights. Something I could never have done without waking them.

Jessie brandished the note I'd written. I pretended to peruse it. "Making fun of an elf's not nice. Laughing sisters must pay the price. Think of a way to undo the damage. Quickly now, my mischief's managed."

Tate let out a pretend wail. "What are we supposed to do?"

"Where's our stuff?" Jessie demanded, not quite as amused as Tate. Knowing the girls would search for their items, they'd gone home with Greg the night before, so there was no way they could find them.

"What do you do when you hurt someone's feelings?" I asked.

"I guess we can apologize," Tate offered.

"I guess you can. Sir Cliff probably took your things to the North Pole when he checked in last night. If he accepts your apologies, I'm guessing he'll return them tomorrow."

"I suspect that Sir Cliff wasn't the one upset by us laughing," Jessie said, giving Greg an appraising look.

I gasped and clasped my hand in front of my mouth. "Surely you don't think Greg would do this?"

"I don't know, Jessie. Mr. Greg isn't one to pull pranks," Tate offered, but she too stared at Greg.

Jessie pursed her lips in thought. "There's always a first time, and he's been dating Mom. She's probably had a horrible effect on him."

"Jessica Elyse! I am not a bad influence," I said between poorly contained laughter.

The girls apologized to both Sir Cliff and Greg.

Greg shrugged it off. "I've never heard of a shelf elf, but it seems like a harmless tradition."

"I hope Sir Cliff's crankiness hasn't put you girls off it," I said.

"As long as we get our stuff back, we're good," Jessie said.

After dinner, Greg snuck the purloined items back to our cottage. I'd return them and hide the elf the following morning.

I set my phone alarm and conked out on the couch. Thanks to the high jinxes of yesterday, I unfortunately slept like a babe.

#

"Nnn-huh," I said, rubbing gritty sleep from my eyes. Then I remembered the elf and the gifts and shot up like a cannon. "Time, time—" My phone had been under my cheek, damp with what I hoped was sweat, but was probably drool. Whew! I had maybe twenty minutes to put the girls' items back and get the elf down. Greg had thoughtfully rigged Sir Cliff so that one string attached to the top of the canopied bed acted as a pulley. All I had to do was untie it or, in the name of expediency, cut it, lower the elf until I could reach him, then unimaginatively stow him on the bathroom shelf.

I'd taken the bag with the necklace and pencils and slipped it into the desk during dinner as surreptitiously as possible, but from the glances, the girls knew what I hid there. I pressed on my phone light, followed the beam to the desk, and opened the door.

The bag was gone!

"Nooo," I moaned. Had it fallen to the bottom? I hastily tossed items out of the drawer into the corner. When I reached the bottom, the drawer was empty.

"Where the heck is it?" I walked in a tight circle. "Stop, Becca, and think." It was possible that Tate wanted to draw after dinner. She could have snuck the bag out and intended to return it before she went to bed, but forgot.

I turned the light off and used the hall and bedroom nightlights to navigate the corridor to the girls' room. Nothing was on the desk. As I tiptoed over to the bed, I stubbed my toe on a book. I clasped my hand over my mouth to muffle a cry of pain. Then I limped the rest of the way to the space between the desk and the girls' beds. Two spots where I often found missing items. Too many shadows darkened the room, and I didn't want to risk the light, so I felt along the floor. I dislodged a disgruntled kitty from Jessie's side.

"What in the world are you doing here?" I asked. She usually slept at the foot of Jessie's bed.

The cat gave a soft merrow as though put out and hopped on the bed to curl up at Jessie's head.

"Okay…" I whispered, shaking my head at her weird behavior. My fingers grappled around Tate's side, but found nothing.

Glancing at the phone, it registered that I had only ten minutes until the girls' alarm went off. I decided to forget the bag until I could ask the girls about it and at least get the elf moved.

There were scissors on the desk glinted in the moonlight. I slipped them from the tray and used the bedpost to guide me up to the top. Standing on tiptoe, I reached up and felt for the string—and found nothing.

If Sir Clifford fell, I would have tripped over him when I went between the girls' beds. I got back on my knees and felt around the floor, even under the girls' beds. (No elf, but quite a bit of dirty laundry.) *Yep, going to broach that topic with the girls first thing in the morning.*

Canopy! Sir Clifford must have dropped on it! Standing as close as I could, I cupped the light and held it over the bed. I wasn't tall enough to see over the top.

I carefully lifted the chair at the desk and scooted it closer to the bed. "I sure hope the girls appreciate the lengths I go to for them," I muttered as I stepped up and cast the light along the top of the canopy. An army of dust bunnies stared back at me. I pointed the phone up toward the ceiling. He wasn't between the lights where we'd hung him!

When I crouched to step down, Tate said, "Mom? What are you doing?"

Startled, I yelped and fell over backwards into Jessie's bed.

"Oof! What the—" Jessie unearthed from a pile of blankets. "Mom?"

Tate switched on the lights.

I rolled upright on the side of Jessie's bed, then stood. "Do you girls know where Sir Cliff is?"

Jessie's laugh turned into a yawn. "Very funny, Mom."

"I'm not kidding, Jess. I can't find him."

"Riiight. He's vanished to the North Pole and is late getting back. Just go on and do whatever you were doing. We'll sleep a little longer." Jess nodded to Tate, and they both curled up on the beds, shut their eyes, and waited.

"Get up!" I insisted.

"Mo-om! The alarm hasn't even gone off yet," Jess complained.

Of course, then the alarm beeped. The girls groaned and rolled out of bed. "I call the bathroom first," Tate said and rushed down the hall.

Jessie regarded me, noting my state. "Hey. Are you okay?"

"I fell asleep on the couch."

"Better call school and tell them we'll be late."

I went to the other side of Jessie's bed and searched between that and the closet.

"Mom, what are you looking for?"

"Sir Clifford!"

"How did you manage to lose him?" Jessie said as she helped me search.

"I don't know. I overslept and came in here to move him, but he was gone."

We'd search for five minutes when Tate returned. "What are you looking for?"

"Sir Clifford," Jess said.

A puzzled expression wrinkled Tate's brow. "He's in the bathroom."

"How'd he get there?" Jessie asked.

I rushed past both the girls and threw open the bathroom door. Sir Clifford Elvin Shaw-Fields straddled the sink faucet as he clutched a tube of toothpaste.

The girls edged in beside me. On the mirror, someone had written in Colgate gel, "BE GOOD." Everyone's toothbrushes laid on the counter, toothpasted and ready for use. Someone had even removed his Harry Potter gear, folded the cape, and set the glasses on top. The broom brush was beside it.

"Cute, Mom," Jess said.

"Girls, I didn't do this."

"Then who did?"

"Maybe Greg? Let's get ready for school. He's coming by for breakfast any minute. It's going to be a Pop-Tarts and juice day. I don't have time to make anything nutritious."

The girls let me get ready first so I could answer the door. I was adding a sweater to my ensemble when I heard a knock.

I opened the door. "Come on in." As I practically herded him inside, I whispered, "Did you move Sir Cliff and the bag with the girls' stuff in it?"

"Nae. Just got here. Didn't you do it before you went to bed?"

"I fell asleep on the couch. When I woke up, the elf vanished. We found him in the bathroom on the sink."

"What was he doing there?" Greg asked.

"Apparently helping us get ready by preparing our toothbrushes and reminding us he'd be watching for any unacceptable behavior. He's even signed his full name."

"That must have taken much toothpaste."

"We're running late. Breakfast is going to be portable. Sorry." I yanked the box of Pop-Tarts from the cabinet and tossed Greg a bag, then stuffed two in my purse to share with the girls at the bus stop. I was rustling around in the refrigerator for juice boxes when the girls came in.

After I plonked the cartons on the table, I yelled, "Hurry up! I think we can make it if we run. I don't want to have to call Kay and ask her to give us a ride." Kay and Amberlee are our closest neighbors. Kay was the first friend I made here.

Jessie pulled out her chair to sit at the table and lace her shoes when she gasped. "Mom, look!" She held up a small present wrapped in toilet paper and strung with a ribbon.

Tate checked her seat and found one, too. They tore open the gifts and quickly discovered their missing items in the crude wrapping.

"But who could have done it?" Tate asked.

Jessie slipped the necklace around her neck and Tate actually put the pencils on the shelf I'd designated for crafts in the linen closet.

"If Sir Cliff gets the girls to put things in their proper places, I'm all for him getting his knickers in a twist," I told Greg, hustling everyone out the door. Greg walked with us to the bus stop. The girls jogged ahead so the bus driver could see them and would hopefully wait.

"Knickers in a twist? Now that's nae something I've heard."

"Something I picked up while living overseas. I guess I should find out exactly where it came from. Americans are bad about incorporating British and Scottish slang without always knowing the exact meaning."

The girls had outgrown many traditions like the Easter Bunny, but some traditions were too dear to let go, and the shelf elf was one of them. I'd hoped that, with Greg's help, we could spice up the elf hiding places, but he wasn't admitting to the prank. If he wasn't responsible for the toothpaste mischief, then someone else was.

The girls swore they didn't move the elf, and I was inclined to believe them. It wasn't even December yet, and I already had a Christmas mystery to solve.

Chapter 2
Becca

"I dinna like it," Greg said, his voice gruff and his brows furrowed.

"Whoever or whatever's doing it isn't hurting anything," I said, as much to assure myself as to assure Greg.

We'd had Sir Clifford out for over a week and the only time I'd placed him was the first two nights. Since then, he'd been moving around, seemingly on his own. I had to admit, he or his conveyors put in a lot more effort in creating adorable spots. So far, we'd found Sir Clifford in every room of the house.

We found connecting snowflakes made of toilet paper cascading from the roll to the floor while Sir Cliff sat on the almost empty roll holding tiny toenail scissors. The next day, someone enclosed him in a transparent balloon surrounded by enough other ones to fill the tub.

One morning he sat on the mantle playing a cardboard guitar. My open eyeglass case, sat sprinkled with Hershey kisses—loot he'd made busking.

The place that took the longest time to discover was the freezer. Tate's Elsa figurine from "Frozen" gestured to Sir Clifford, frozen in an oversized ice cube. The next day rivaled all previous days when we found him inside an unopened cereal box.

\#

As we decorated our tree, I told Greg stories about the ornaments. He had brought a supply of candy canes and as the girls sat stringing popcorn, their red striped treats hung from their mouths like straws.

We studded oranges with cloves, and I heated apple cider to perfume the house. Having far too many decorations for the small cottage, we had to be selective

I thought we had another mystery to solve when the bows kept disappearing off the gifts. We discovered them in the oddest places, like beneath the bathtub faucet, on the kitchen counter, or under the rocking chair. Then we caught our wee fuzzy bow thief, tail held high, standing on the top tier of the cat tree, with his paws ensnared in a bow twice his size. Seeing as the cat was out of the bag, Tabby leaped for the lower rung, but tripped and somersaulted off the post. Embarrassed, but unharmed, she fled to Jessie for comfort.

The day after we put up the tree, we found Sir Cliff, his face colored with green camo, hiding on the top limb—thankfully, whoever did it used a water-color marker. Next the mysterious movers ensconced him on the sofa with popcorn, coke and the remote for movie night—which was creepy because we really *had* a Christmas movie night planned to introduce Greg to *A Christmas Story.*

One night, they stuffed the elf in a large envelope stamped and addressed to us, leaving it on the floor beneath the mail slot.

This morning we woke up to kitty meowing and rolling on the floor trying to get the elf off her back.

I'd assumed by now someone would have owned up to the elf mischief, but no one did

"You should put that elf where no one can get to it," Greg insisted.

"But the girls are having so much fun," I protested. So was I, for that matter. It was nice to have these light, silly moments in our lives instead of the usual stresses of the fae world attacking us directly, like when vampire fae tried to drink our blood, or indirectly, like the recent changeling conflict.

Greg folded his arms in front of his chest. "Tonight, I'm staying up. I'll find out who this sneak is."

"Okay, but I'm staying up with you."

I petted the kitten and waited for it to calm down before unwinding the rest of the ribbon someone had used to tie Sir Clifford aboard. That night, the girls wanted to stay up too, but I sent them to bed. I shut the kitty in the girls' room with water and a litter box. As for Sir Clifford, we set the elf on the couch between us. I felt like I was being chaperoned, but no way would anyone be able to get to Sir Clifford without one of us knowing.

Since we were essentially staking out the cottage, we couldn't enjoy activities we normally would if left alone. We shared a couple of kisses, but Sir Clifford just made it a little too weird to enjoy—that, and knowing as it got darker, someone was poised to sneak in.

The later it got, the harder it was to keep my eyes opened. I kept tipping over and bumping Greg's shoulder.

Finally, he said, "Rebecca, go to sleep."

I must have dropped off because I woke up to the sound of Greg's yelp. "What's wrong?"

"I ken whose been moving the elf!"

The girls' bedroom door squeaked, heralding their arrival. The girls peeked in, mouths agape.

Greg turned toward them. "It's nae problem."

"Grown-ups are so weird sometimes," Tate said as the girls went back to the bedroom.

I turned to Greg. "Okay. Are you going to tell me what you saw?" Then I noticed Sir Cliff had vanished from the spot between us. "Where's the elf?" I tugged up the pillows, looking.

"He's nae here, but I'm sure the girls will find him when they wake tomorrow morning."

"What's going on?" Then I noticed his hair. I reached up to finger the tiny braid and chuckled. "Who did this?"

"Dinna laugh too hard. You've got two," he informed me. I reached up and, sure enough, I found two braids. One on each side of my head.

After he explained who had been moving Sir Cliff, I said, "I know you're upset, but I think we should just let it go. It'll be Christmas soon enough and time to put Sir Cliff up until next year."

"You mean to just leave the hiding to them?"

"It's not hurting anything and they've done a much better job with it than I ever did. It's actually a relief that someone else is taking over the task. Have you had to send them back every day since this started?"

"Nae. It's not woken me. I guess they've been in and out so fast that I never even knew they left. I've caught them a few times during the day, though."

"Come on, Greg. It's almost Christmas," I pleaded.

"I guess I can leave them to their mischief, at least this time, for the sake of a peaceful holiday."

"Good. I'm pooped and going to bed. You can sleep here."

"Nae. I'm off to my own bed. Good night, Rebecca."

We kissed and after he left, I locked the door and stumbled to bed to get a few hours sleep.

Chapter 3

Tate

The snow was really coming down, and Jessie and I were going to make a snowman. We wanted him to be as traditional as possible—very Frosty, so I went to ask Mrs. Nivens if she had any old men's hats, scarves, and gloves. Mrs. Nivens hired me to help make an inventory of her belongings.

"Goodness Tate. I thought we agreed to stop until after the holidays," said Dorcas, Mrs. Nivens's caregiver when she opened the door.

"We did. I just came to ask Mrs. Nivens a favor."

"She's in the parlor. Let me make sure she's ready for guests."

I sat on the bench just outside the entrance, across from a creepy mirror. Whenever I glanced at it from the corner of my eye, I always swore I could see someone in it. I didn't think that someone was very happy.

Dorcas returned. "She's thrilled she can help someone. It's hard on her—aging and feeling worthless."

"She's far from worthless. I think she's one of the most interesting people I've ever met."

"Well, you be sure to tell her that."

I followed Dorcas into the parlor. "Hello, Tate." Mrs. Nivens sat on her usual chair. She had a box of old photos.

"Hi, Mrs. Nivens. Are you going up to your sister's for Christmas?"

"No, she thinks I'm getting too old for the trip, so she and some of the family will celebrate Christmas here." Mrs. Nivens frowned.

"That should be nice. You've got plenty of rooms for visitors and you won't have to pack. You'll have everything you need here."

"That's what I told them. But they're just coming down for Christmas Day. Then they're leaving. But enough about an old lady's complaints. What can I do for you?"

I explained what I wanted and why.

"Check in the attic. There are probably enough old clothes up there to give every person in Thistle a complete wardrobe," Mrs. Nivens said.

"I'll show you what I've found, so I don't put anything valuable on the snowman."

"Those garments and such have been up there so long that the moths and Old Man Time probably have made them worthless. Show me, though. I'd like to see what survived and if I recognize any of it. Wouldn't it be wonderful if we found the dress that my great grandmother wore in this portrait?" Mrs. Nivens pointed to the photo album on her lap. "I should add great, great great to grandmother, but I'm old and don't have time for such nonsense."

A portrait over the fireplace caught my eye. It displayed a young woman in a blue gown with dark hair the shade of Mrs. Nivens's nephew, Conall's. Intricate lace spilled from the sleeves and what looked like some sort of underskirt. "Who is that?"

"That, my dear, is the original lady of the manor, Aurinda McNeil. Her name means gold and both her husband and she, via inheritance, were quite wealthy. I think the dress she's wearing is called a robe a la francaise, but I'm far from a historical clothing expert."

I walked closer. "There's so much detail," I said, admiring the satin bows and tassels on the skirt and the gold buttons and embroidery on the bodice. "What happened to her?"

"They say she left him. I think Old Mister was a monster."

"A monster!?"

Mrs. Nivens patted her leg. Her chuckle turned into a dry cough.

I grabbed a lozenge from one of the porcelain dishes, a cat one, quickly unwrapped it and gave it to her.

"Not a wolf, like everyone believes. Just the garden variety cruel man who should have never married nor had children. She was a grand woman. But despite her wealth, she hadn't the power to keep her children. He held onto them not so much because he cared about them, but more because he just didn't want her to have them." Mrs. Nivens struggled to her feet.

I quickly took her arm.

"Watch her as we walk in front of the painting. Her eyes seem to follow."

Dark blue eyes watched me as I helped Mrs. Nivens across the floor to the sofa. "What happened to her?"

"Who knows? She vanished and since she wasn't a part of the McNeil clan any longer, time and willful neglect swallowed her up."

"That's sad. How could she just disappear?"

"Not a clue. She didn't even pack."

I wondered if the fae had anything to do with her disappearance. Or maybe, her husband really *was* a monster like a werewolf. "How do you know so much?"

"It's odd. The pieces of history a family keeps and those they choose to forget." In that moment, Mrs. Nivens's mouth caved in on itself. I saw her as she would be in her coffin. Her mood turned melancholy. "Tell me young Tate, do you think, a few generations hence, anyone will remember me?"

"I'll always remember you. And my mother will too. And I bet your nephews won't forget you."

Mrs. Nivens smiled. "I'm glad to know it, child." She turned away. "Dorcas!"

Dorcas rushed in. "What's wrong?"

"I'm ready for one of those naps you always say I need. Help me to the bedroom."

"Yes?" Dorcas gingerly took Mrs. Niven's arm and helped her rise.

"Mind you, take young Tate up to the attic. She has a project I've promised to help her with."

"Yes, ma'am."

I sat alone in the room. I didn't know what occurred exactly, but I knew it was important.

The attic was a mess, but Mrs. Nivens's prediction about the quality of the items up there proved to be incorrect. Someone was very careful when packing the trunks, wardrobes, and cupboards.

I easily found clothes. The problem was finding ones I wouldn't feel awful about leaving outside in the snow. An hour passed, and while it was enjoyable, it wasn't productive.

I closed the door on a gorgeous silk dress and left to find Dorcas enjoying a cup of tea.

"Any luck?" she asked.

"There are a lot of clothes, but everything's way too fancy to use on my snowman." I sat across from Dorcas, leaning an elbow on the table and using one hand to prop up my chin. She gestured to the teapot, and I nodded.

"Let me look in what used to be the servants' quarters. I'll find something suitable."

"If you tell me where, I can look. I know Mrs. Nivens keeps you busy."

"Thank you, Tate."

The clothes were scattered between several rooms and, thanks to the lack of organization, it took me just as long as the attic search, but I finally found the items I was looking for. I unearthed one battered hat, what looked like gardening gloves caked with mud, two galoshes that weren't the same size, and a faded striped scarf long enough to wrap twice around my waist.

"Do you think it's okay if I take these without showing them to Mrs. Nivens since I didn't get them from the attic? I don't want to wake her."

"I'm sure it's fine," Dorcas said.

I examined the hat. "What's wrong with the rim?"

"That, my dear, is a tricorn."

"Isn't that like a pirate hat?"

"Yes, but not all tricorns have the sides completely up against the crown. This one's more useful. I'm sure the servant tugged on the brim enough to reshape it, too. What are you going to do with the wellies?"

"I've got an idea. I just have to convince Jessie."

"Sounds mysterious." She smiled at me, her eyes twinkling with interest. "I'll have to drop by your cottage to see what you've built. Give us a ring so we can come see it before it melts."

"I will." I turned to leave, but a thought occurred to me. "Dorcus, I have an idea." When I outlined my plan, Dorcas agreed to help.

#

I showed Jessie my finds from Mrs. Nivens. "Perfect! But why the galoshes? They aren't even the same size."

"They're close enough." I shrugged. "Before we go out, I'm going to draw him so we don't waste time standing there freezing."

I drew my snowman idea and showed Jess.

"I like it. Our snowman will be the coolest one on the Shrouded Isle."

"It's a pity that it'll melt."

"Yeah." Jessie rubbed her chin and gazed off into space, her expression pensive. She abruptly stood and reached for the spell book. "I've got an idea."

An hour later, we were up to our knees in the snow, making our snowman. We built him in the front yard but rolled the snow from the side and to the back of the house. It was the one area of the yard we had walked on the least. It worked even better than we thought and by the time we rolled the balls from the back of the house to the front, the size was perfect. When we finished, we called Mom out.

"No wonder it's taken you two so long."

"What do you think?" I asked.

Getting the scarf on him was the biggest challenge. His legs are a little too short, but I doubted anyone would notice since they'll focus on how our snowman differed from everybody else's. We'd used a carrot for his nose and two walnuts for his eyes. For his mouth, we used a broken bracelet with large, red beads. Mom taught us the trick of dipping the pieces in salty water so they'd stick better.

"I think it's wonderful. Whatever made you think of building a snowman standing on his head?"

Jess threw an arm around me and squeezed. "Tate designed him and borrowed the outfit from Mrs. Nivens."

Mom tsked. "Pity we'll lose it when the snow melts."

Jessie had taken care of that by finding an incantation to keep him from becoming a puddle of water. I smiled and hoped her spell worked.

"I'm freezing!" Jessie said. "I'm going inside and taking a warm bath."

Mom waved for me to come in. "Come on, Tate. You can help me with hot chocolate."

I ran to the room to dry off and change while Mom collected the ingredients. Our mother may not cook, but she makes great hot cocoa.

As she measured the ingredients, she asked, "Are you ready for Christmas?"

"Pretty much. Are you?" I asked.

Mom sighed. "No, I have a few more things to get. The gift I'm most worried about is the one for Greg."

"Are you having trouble thinking of something to get him?"

"You know about his razor?" Mom asked.

"Yes. It looks more like a weapon, though."

One side of Mom's mouth quirked up. "I think so too, but he likes to use it and was glad when I found it and returned it to him. He usually shaves with just water and though he's good with the straight edge, he occasionally nicks himself." Mom whisked the ingredients together. "I did some research—"

I interrupted, to say, "Of course," then grinned.

Mom nudged me with her elbow. "Yes. And I found out that back in the late 1700s, they had shaving kits. So, I visited the antiques store on the mainland, but the proprietor said they didn't have any."

"Uh oh. What are you going to get him instead?"

"The man said he didn't have any *now*, but he'll check around with his contacts. And true to his word, he did."

"Did he find any?"

"Yes, but it hasn't arrived yet, and I'm worried that it won't get here in time. I've got an emergency gift, but it isn't as nice as the shaving kit."

"And you can't get one anywhere else? We could take the bus to a larger town."

"I called antique shops in Edinburgh and Glasgow."

"Any luck."

Mom's mouth twisted. "Yes, but they were too expensive for me to afford. As it is, I'm going to sell that designer blouse that I've never worn."

I raised my eyebrows in shock. "Wow. Shaving kits must cost heaps."

Mom shook her head and let out a wistful sigh. "Really old ones do."

"Hey, I thought you were going to wear the blouse on Christmas."

"I was, but I have other clothes. Anyway, none of my slacks or skirts match it, so I would have had to wear jeans. And I kinda wanted to be a little more dressy."

"Since it's your first Christmas with Greg?"

"Since it's the first Christmas that we put out all the Christmas decorations since your dad died. Last year we just exchanged gifts."

"It's an awfully pretty blouse, though."

"It is. But I'd rather get Greg something special than wear a ridiculously expensive blouse I'd worry about staining. I wouldn't be able to enjoy myself for fear of dribbling cider down it."

"Mom?"

"Yes, honey?"

"When I was at Mrs. Nivens, she told me that her family didn't think she was well enough to take a trip down south."

"Is she going to be alone? She can always come here, though we'll be cramped for space. I'll ask Kay to pick her up."

"No, her relatives are coming here, but they aren't spending the night. They're only coming down to visit and open gifts, then they're leaving. She seems sad about it."

"I imagine so. No one wants to be alone for the Christmas holidays. Dorcas is likely to be with her."

"I didn't ask, but I suppose so." Remembering the house, I realized there wasn't even a wreath on the door. "There aren't any holiday decorations at Mrs. Nivens's."

"She is too frail to manage it and they hired Dorcas to take care of her, not put up a Christmas tree and mistletoe."

"True. Maybe we could take a couple of decorations over. Our cottage is too small and we have so many that we're not even using."

"That's a good idea, Tate." Mom kissed the top of my head. "Why don't we look around and see what might work best?"

By the time Jessie got out of the bath, we had a generous mound of Christmas decorations in the middle of the living room hall.

"What are you doing?" she asked.

Mom looked up from unboxing ornaments. "We're going to go to Mrs. Nivens and decorate her house."

I explained about Mrs. Nivens's relatives and our idea.

"Don't go yet. Gavin got their tree from the mainland. He said you'd have to be barmy to hack one down on the island. The man who owned the place was friendly. He has some trees that just aren't selling because they have bare spots, and he was going to take them to the dump. Gavin and I can see if he'll donate one."

Gavin, Jessie's boyfriend, was nice and didn't treat me like a child. "Good idea."

Chapter 4

Greg

"Rebecca?" I'd just finished a sweep around the perimeter of the forest checking for rogue fae. 'Twas a late one for me, but with the holidays coming, I didna want to be accused of negligence if something amiss happened. Something is amiss now. I could feel it in my bones, but I dinna understand it.

"What? Is something wrong?" she asked as she closed the shed door. The cold had turned her cheeks the shiny red of an apple and her hair hung in pretty ringlets. She dinna like her hair and says it's a boring color and frizzy. But I look and I see the colors of the forest in her long tresses. The strands of gray she laments just add to her beauty, glistening like silver amongst the mahogany, sienna, hazel, and chocolate browns. When she frees her curls and the locks dance in the wind, she looks fairy-kissed.

"Greg? I asked you if something was wrong." She laid her cool hand on my arm.

"Aye." I said like a dreamy gowk. "I dinna know." I added gruffly. "Let's go inside. Your lips are chapped."

She licked them, not knowing what the sight did to me. "I'll put some lip balm on them."

I cleared my throat. "Aye."

She bustled through the grass, her hips swaying. I was happy to follow.

When we got inside, I prepared tea while she put on her lip softener and did whatever else women do when they excused themselves.

"Oh, thanks." She warmed her hands on the mug. "You're early for dinner. The girls aren't even home. I'll get something started in a minute."

"Aye. I'm early and food can wait."

"Uh oh. Just give me the news."

"I havena said anything, because whatever I've been seeing isna a fae. You ken?"

She nodded.

"I've seen something white in the forest."

"What does it look like?"

"I canna tell you more than that. I canna get close to it. Fast it is."

"Is it tall? Wide? Could it be a snowshoe rabbit? Do you even have those here?"

"We have mountain hare that turn white in the cold, but it isna it. It's too large."

"Maybe a dog snuck over on the ferry?"

"Aye. It would have to be a large one, you ken? The stories about the white wolf—"

"You think?"

"Nae. Not really. But since I saw it, I've asked around. And Mr. Samms and Kay have both seen it."

"Did they get close enough to tell what kind of animal it was?"

"Mr. Samms said it looked like a polar bear."

"There're no bears in Scotland and even when there were, I'm sure there were no polar bears. Maybe the changelings?"

In the fall, the fae queen sent two changelings to cause mischief, but they vanished and we hadna trouble with them since. "This is larger than a child, but no as big as a man."

"Hmm, I guess the only thing we can do is keep watch."

Rebecca had a board stretched out in front of her. She'd draped a blouse on top of it. I'd nae seen one exactly like that yonder, but I'd watched my wife at laundering and ken an iron when I saw it. "New blouse?"

"No. Well, I got it before I left the States. The iron's out since I needed it for what I'm wearing to Kay's, so I thought I'd get the wrinkles out of it too. I think she invited the entire village."

"I've nae been to a solstice party."

"Kay says she's going all out since it's the first one she's had with Amberlee. She said they planned on veering a bit from druid tradition and will add some traditions from other cultures because, as she said, 'why not?'"

"Humph. As long as there's no dancin' around scuddies, I'm good."

It took her a minute to ken what I meant. "Oh, no. I'm sure everyone will wear clothes, even Mr. McVitie, if he even comes."

The male selkie was usually very gruff, but when he let his hair down, so to speak, he'd been known to go skinny dipping. "I ken he will."

"Really?"

"Aye. Dorcas is coming."

"Hm."

I recognized that glint. Women canna resist match-making. "I dinna know if it's like that, but I do know they dinna need shoved together."

"Apparently, they're both doing fine on their own. And no, I wasn't trying to pair the two up."

She picked up the blouse and put it on a hanger, then sighed. "It's pretty, but I have nothing that really goes with it."

"The color's braw. You'd look bonny wearing it with the Gillie tartan."

Rebecca smiled. "I'd love to have a skirt made of your tartan, but I don't know how to sew. I'd have to hire someone. Maybe someday—"

It was at that moment I decided someday would be this Christmas.

#

Thistle had a shop that sold kilts and such, so I dinna need to go to the mainland. 'Twas just as weil. I still wasna used to the noise. Too hoachin for me. When I walked in, a ding rang, but I dinna see a bell over the door.

"I'll be right with you," someone yelled from the back. The tartans were labeled and in alphabetical order, but when I got to "Gillie," it wasna correct.

"I wondered how long it'd be before I saw you." The man, unlike most of the villagers, was clad in a proper kilt, though a wee shorter than the ones I was used to. He was bright as a peacock on its way to a ball. "Yer kilt wearin' oot?" He asked with a flourish of hands.

"Nae. I'm looking for the Gillie tartan, but it isna here."

The man strode down the aisle. "Aye, it is." He went to tug the bolt out.

"Gonny no dae that," I said, pressing the bolt back into place. "Dinna you know your plaids? That isna the Gillie tartan."

The shopkeeper stepped back so he could look up at me. "It is now."

"What?" I struggled to keep my temper. "I'm a Gillie. I ken me own tartan and that isna it."

"Things have changed since you went into the forest." He fingered the dark, drab plaid. "This here is the modern Gillie tartan."

"Well, I dinna like it and I willna wear it! Dinna you have the proper one?"

The man heaved a sigh, traipsed back down the aisle, and ducked behind the counter. He tugged an enormous book from beneath it and flipped through the pages until he found the right one. "Is this what yer wantin'?"

I turned the book toward me. Two samples of cloth were stapled to the page and the name 'Gillie' labeled the page. "Aye. I'll be wanting this one." I ran my finger down the finely woven design of blue, gold, and cream with a touch of red. Thin lines of forest green ran through it. The exact color of Rebecca's bonny blouse.

"Enough for a kilt?"

"Nae." I tried to think of the most manly way of saying I needed it for a skirt and decided there wasna one. "Rebecca dinna have a proper tartan skirt. I'm buying the tartan for that—unless you have one already made?" I asked hopefully.

"Nae," he said right back at me.

When he told me the price, I didna know whether to laugh or smack at the wee bampot. "Yer off yer heid!"

Noting my mood, the man said, "Now, dinna get angry. Look for yerself." He pointed at numbers beneath the cloth. "Do ye want me to order it?"

"Aye."

"It will come in about two weeks."

"It better." I stomped to the door.

"And ye better have the money!" he shouted at me.

I could never make that much money in the time before Christmas. Then I had an idea. I wasna sure if it would work and I'd have to ask Jessie if she could help me find the right place, but I had to try.

Chapter 5
Jessie

As the weather warmed up, Tate and I kept checking the snowman. My spell must have worked! He wasn't getting any smaller. However, somebody must have come right up to him at night because there were footsteps all around him. I could follow them up the lane, but they disappeared where our lane joined Thistle's main road. At least the person did nothing to him, but I could swear he moved.

After snowing all night, the next day, the same thing happened. I found footsteps around the snowman, but this time, the steps led into the forest.

When I came inside, I asked Mom, "Has Greg found anything odd in the forest lately?"

"Not really. He says that the only fae out and about are the weakest ones. He's been on the lookout for changelings, but no one's seen any strange children around. Kay drew a picture of what the two we know look like, so if they come back, the villagers can tell us."

"I've been noticing footsteps around the snowman. They appear almost every day."

"It's a clever idea for a snowman to be built upside down. Maybe somebody wanted to get a closer look to see how you and Tate constructed it."

"But if a different person makes the footsteps every time, that's a lot of people prowling around our yard at night."

"True. Why don't you ask your friends? I just can't see adults being so fascinated by a snowman that they'd sneak over to look at it."

I sighed. The only person I hung out with these days was Gavin. I'd gotten off on the wrong foot with the kids on the island right off the bat. Gavin and I immediately hit it off. Unfortunately, a lot of the girls had crushes on him and resent that he was interested in me instead of them. Then there's Lundy. He's a relative of Mrs. Nivens and Conall. He had a crush on me and was insufferable. He followed me around and claimed I was with him at a ceilidh, when I wanted nothing to do with him. (They had to explain to me that ceilidh was just another word for party.) So, I played a trick on him that backfired and ruined an outing for everyone. I don't even want to imagine what they think of me now that Grace, a classmate, has been asleep for weeks thanks to the Sleeping Beauty curse a fae cast. It wasn't my fault, but I bet they blame me all the same. Mom mentioned that a family with a daughter around my age would move here, but it would only be temporary and who's to say that she would like me?

"Jess?"

"Yes, Mom?"

"We really need to bring something over to Kay and Amberlee's house tonight. Do you think you could make cookies?"

I was excited about going because they'd planned some sort of druid celebration that included a lot of different customs. It should be fun.

"I guess. Do you want any particular kind?"

"I don't know. I guess something druid-like?"

"Not very helpful, Mom." I love my mom dearly, but she's not the best cook. So, I often take up the slack.

"Here. Choose something. Anything. Go into town and buy what you need."

She handed me a couple of bills. "Look online or in one of the cookbooks I've got—"

"That you never use." I grinned.

"Yes, smarty pants." She smiled back.

"What time are we supposed to be there?"

"Seven."

I'd make gingerbread men. We'd done it at a friend's house, and it seemed pretty easy. Mom even had cookie cutters that I'd never seen her use. I think she got them as a wedding gift ages ago, before I was even born.

I peeked into our bedroom. My sister was reading on her bed. "Hey Tate? Do you want to go into town with me?"

She shoved a book under the pillow. I think maybe she was keeping a diary because I'd seen her writing in it too. I dunno why she'd hide it. It's not like I'd ever read it

Tate bounced from the bed. "Sure. I have some things I want to get for the ornaments I'm making."

Tate was really good with crafts. I didn't really have the patience for it. I did like spell making, and in a way, it's the same. You have directions you need to follow to get what you want. I guess I just liked the idea of doing magic better. It's something that not everyone can do. Anyone can pile cinnamon sticks together and tie a bow around them. Well, if anyone really wanted to.

Tate and I found almost everything we needed at the grocery.

Lundy was there working for his uncle Conall. As usual. "Hi Jessie."

"Hi Lundy." I was trying to be nicer. And I guess he was trying not to be so irritating.

"Are you going to the winter solstice party?" he asked, to my surprise.

I'd thought it was going to be a small gathering with just, well, us, but I guess Amberlee and Kay were going all out. "Yes. I'm going to make cookies to bring."

"I've been gathering mistletoe and holly for them. My uncle's bringing three bottles of wine."

"Cool. If you're invited, Gavin is probably coming too. I guess I'll see you there."

It didn't take long to gather the ingredients, and we were back at the bus stop in time to catch the next bus. I'd gotten pretty good at predicting how much time it would take to do stuff in town, and had the bus schedule down pat. It stinks when you're ready to leave and the bus just left.

"What are you going to do about the decorating?" Tate asked as the bus pulled up.

"I'll call Kay. Maybe she has tools to make lines on cookies."

"Even if she does, you've never done it before."

"I won't be doing anything fancy, just the mouths and maybe the lines around the necks, wrists and ankles to show where the clothes are."

When we reached the cottage, footprints were scattered around the front of the house.

Tate stared at the snowman. "Has he moved a little closer to the porch?"

"He's made of snow, Tate," I said, rolling my eyes. "I'd sure like to know who keeps coming around and traipsing through our yard."

#

The dough had to chill for at least three hours. After I had put two large balls of dough in the refrigerator. I went to see what Tate was working on.

"I've never had gingerbread. Do you think your cookies will taste good?" she asked as she tied a bow around a bunch of cinnamon sticks.

"I hope so. When we made the men at my friend's, the dough was white."

"What made the dough dark?"

"The molasses mostly. The spices too."

"The molasses looked icky," Tate commented. As she concentrated, the tip of her tongue peeked out.

I didn't tell her, but I'd tasted the molasses and it *was* nasty. I thought it would taste like honey. Blech! "People always talk about gingerbread men, so they must taste good—or at least okay."

Tate had a batch of orange slices baking in the oven. When they dried out, we'd poke holes in the top and thread ribbons through. Then we could tie them and use them to hang the slices on the tree.

I texted Gavin, and he said Kay invited his family to the winter solstice celebration too. When I explained about Mrs. Nivens, Gavin offered to call the tree seller. He and his dad would drive the truck over to get a tree and deliver it. Gavin's dad didn't think it would be a good idea to leave the task until the last minute, so he offered to pay for the tree if the man didn't have any he wanted to give away.

I called Kay and asked her about the icing.

"What are you making?"

"Gingerbread men. The dough's in the refrigerator, so I don't need it right away."

"I have a recipe for an easy white icing. Cut the tip off a plastic bag, put the icing inside, and you can squeeze it out to make lines and simple decorations."

"I made a double batch of dough. We're going to make some more for Mrs. Nivens. She's having her family over for Christmas this year and can't really do much to decorate and cook. It's a surprise." I told her about the tree, ornaments, and everything else we planned.

"I can help with the ornaments and I've got a wreath already made. Do you know what else she needs?"

"Not really. It was Tate's idea."

"I'll call Dorcas and see what she suggests, then I'll call around and see who can donate anything we still need to make the day wonderful for her and her family. Tell your mom so she doesn't do extra work."

"Okay. Thanks."

I needed the entire table to make the cookies. I'd just put the first batch in the oven when I saw a shadow. I turned, expecting Mom.

"Yikes" I yelled. Greg stood directly behind me. "Why didn't you knock?"

"I didna want to make noise."

"Mom's out back."

"I ken. I need a favor."

What in the world would he want from me? "Oo-kay."

"I've ordered tartan for your mom so she can have a skirt made to match that fancy blouse she has."

"That's... nice."

"I dinna know anything about how much she'll need and I was hoping you could tell me."

"What kind of skirt do you want made?"

"Uh. A skirt. Like a kilt. But fancy and for a woman." Greg's hair was tied back, but strands hung out like he had been running his hands over his head, and the tips of his ears pinked.

"I know Mom likes pockets."

"Pockets?! A kilt dinna have pockets." Greg paced the floor as he gripped the sides of his head. "I bet that Thistle shopkeeper ordered the wrong amount!"

"What shopkeeper?" I asked.

"The one in the village!" His voice boomed in exasperation.

"Calm down!"

"But I want to get your mum something nice. And now that git's ordered the wrong thing. I havena money to pay for it!"

"First, are you talking about the kilts shop in the village?" He nodded. "Let me call them for you. Maybe they can hold the order."

I used the landline and found the number in one of the pamphlets Mom collected.

"Tartans and More, Ian speaking."

"Hi. I'm Jessie Shaw. I'm calling for Greg Gillie. He was just there to order tartan for a skirt. I think there might have been a misunderstanding—"

The shopkeeper laughed. "Not on my part."

I took a deep breath. I was beginning to understand Greg's frustration. "He wants to order material to make my mom a long skirt with pockets. A-line, I think it's called, but I'm going to call our friend, Kay, to make sure."

"Aye, Kay would know. She's a fine seamstress."

"So, the tartan you ordered. Is it the right kind?"

"Aye. The lad thought he wanted wool, but I ordered the right fabric. And you tell him I ordered the right bloody pattern too!"

"So, you got fabric that can be made into the kind of skirt I described?"

"That's just what I said, lassie!"

Geez. "I'm calling Kay. I'll call you back."

"Dinna make me no never mind. It's ordered and the laddie better have enough money to pay for it. Now I've got a customer. Good bye."

Greg, his expression troubled, reached for my arm, but stopped short. "What did he say?"

"He hung up on me!"

"Didna I tell you! The man's a bampot!"

"A what?"

"Never mind."

Huh. I'd ask Gavin about it later. I rang Kay. "I'm really sorry to bother you again, but Greg's here and he's all upset."

"I'm nae upset!" he protested.

I shook my head at him and put my finger to my lips.

"What's wrong?" Kay asked.

"He's ordered tartan to have a skirt made for Mom. A fancy, long one with pockets. Do you have any idea how much material that would take and what kind it needs? We aren't sure about wool."

Kay sighed. "I think I know what he wants. I've made one before. I'm going to text you a photo to show him. Hopefully, it'll go through."

When my cell phone beeped, I showed Greg the photo Kay had sent. "This? Is this what you want?"

"Aye."

I rang Kay back. "Greg says, Aye."

"I'll call Ian and explain. I've worked with him before. Once the material arrives, I can make the skirt."

Before she rang off, she told me how much just the tailoring and material cost. *Gulp.*

"Did you check on the price of the material?" I asked Greg.

"Aye." He studied his nails.

"That's a lot of money!" It just burst out of me. "I mean. You don't really have a monthly salary coming in and, well—"

"You're wondering how I can afford it."

"Yeah."

"I'm selling my straight razor. It's considered an antique, and I'll make plenty to take care of your mom's gift." I opened my mouth, but he continued. "Aye. It's time I caught up with the times."

"It's your stuff to do with what you want." Mom said he had been shaving with a knife before she found his razor. He must be desperate to sell it.

"Not a word to your mother."

#

As I packed the cookies, Mom oohed and aahed over them. Honestly, she could do this if she wanted. Then again, I could make ornaments like Tate and I don't. Sometimes, I guess it all comes down to what you want to do.

"Lundy said that he's coming too," I told her.

"Lundy's invited? I thought there'd be mostly adults." Mom fingered her shirt and glanced back at the bedroom.

"Yeah, me too."

Greg showed up, and we were ready to go.

We could see Fables Cottage from the main road. They'd lined the entire path with little sacks illuminated with candles and we could hear festive music as we neared the door.

I knew Gavin would be here, but I didn't know his brother's band would be playing. Disappointment dampened my festive mood. The band members would have Gavin toting amps and mics and supplying them with water bottles throughout the event. I'd hoped tonight—would be, well, our night.

Gavin and I have been seeing each other since this summer and I work part time in his father's stables with the horses. But we're never alone. I mean *never*.

I think I love Gavin. The way I've felt when we hold hands or we've stolen a few kisses—it makes me tingle. It *must* be love. Why else do I fall asleep thinking about him? His voice. The way he smells. His lips. His hands.

I'd like to be alone with him. Just the two of us. We wouldn't—you know, but it would be nice to kiss without worrying my sister was going to walk in or his dad was going to call him for help.

"Jessie? Stop dawdling!" Mom yelled and I could feel my deceitful, fair skin warm.

"Coming," I called back. A beautiful wreath hung on Kay's front door and I could see snow sculptures off to one side of the cottage.

The door opened before we even arrived. Amberlee's face brightened when she saw us.

Mom smiled and hugged her. "The candles are beautiful, Amberlee!"

Amberlee ducked her head. She liked to change up her hair. Tonight, she'd spent extra time on her center part. "Th-thank you." Her shy nature caused a stutter when she got nervous, but Amberlee is the best. Not only is she a talented witch, but she's also so smart. This party must be really stressing her out.

"Someday, you need to teach me how to do that zigzag," I said, motioning to her hair, then hugging her.

"Any time, Jess," she said, with no stutter.

When I found Gavin, his eyes were already on me. The music, the talking—it all faded away. Mom said something, and I nodded mechanically. The path between Gavin and I seemed to open. My eyes never left his.

"Hey."

His face lit up, and I didn't need a mirror to know mine did, too. He took my coat. "You look great, but you always do."

And that is why he's my boyfriend. "So, what do you know about this winter solstice deal?" I asked, trying to go for nonchalant and ignoring my body's zing.

He sighed and rolled his shoulders. "This is the first time Kay has had a party. I guess it's because Amberlee's here."

"Yeah." I watched as Kay squeezed Amberlee's hands and nodded encouragingly back at the door. "They're a great couple."

Gavin jerked his hand out of mine. "What?"

"They're a great couple?"

"You mean like... they... well... they?" He lifted his hands up in the air as if that helped.

"Well, yeah. They're in love."

"But. They're both girls."

Huh? "They're both women." I wanted to say more, but we'd been having issues lately and I'd hoped tonight would be... special. The last thing I wanted to do was argue about Kay and Amberlee. I wasn't sure exactly what Gavin had planned so we could spend time alone, but he had assured me he had a plan.

He shook his head. "Yes, they're women." The band struck up a song that I actually knew how to dance to. He held his hand out to me. "Dance?"

I forced myself not to sound like a love-struck dummy. "Sure."

After dancing several songs, we sat on chairs pushed up against the walls.

Gavin was quickly summoned to help the band, so I was on my own when Tate sat beside me.

"I overheard Mom and Greg talking yesterday," she said.

"You've gotten really nosy lately, haven't you?"

"Do you want to know what they were saying or not?"

"So, what's this news you overheard?"

"It's about Sir Clifford."

"What about him?"

"Mom's not the one hiding him each night."

"So? Greg's doing it."

"Nope."

"Are you doing it? Wait, that doesn't make sense unless Mom and Greg found out?"

"Nope."

"So, who's doing it?"

"That's just it. I don't know. I just overheard them talking about the latest place we found the elf and they were saying how clever the hiding place was. So, obviously, neither one of them has been doing it."

"Okay. That's weird. Who do you think *is* doing it?"

Tate shrugged. "I don't know, but don't you want to find out?"

"I guess. What did you have in mind?"

Tate's eyes lit up. "We stay up and steal Sir Cliff."

"I don't know. What about the penalty for touching him?"

"He's got to be touched by whoever's been moving him. They aren't penalizing themselves. At least I assume not. So why should we get in trouble? It's our elf, not theirs."

"If we move it, then they won't be able to hide it. They probably will just give up."

"I don't think so. This person's got to be pretty sneaky and smart."

"Do you think it's Kay?"

Tate shook her head. "Maybe. I just can't figure out why Mom and Mr. Greg would be okay with anybody else doing it."

"Christmas is only a few days away. We have little time, so if we're going to find out who's doing it, we need to come up with a good plan."

"Okay. How about we don't steal Sir Cliff? We can take turns watching him."

"Then we're going to be exhausted the next day."

"We're out for winter break soon, so it should be okay. I think you should set up your phone to record, too."

"Why don't we just do that and not stay up?"

"Because it will be dark and nothing will show up."

"What if the person just never shows up?"

"I wish we knew how they're getting inside. Do you think Mom leaves the door open for them and then locks it the next morning?"

"No clue."

Gavin brought a glass of punch for me. When he saw Tate, he said, "You can have mine if you want and I can go back for another."

Tate hopped up. "That's okay. Jessie, think about it, okay?"

"Sure."

"What's going on?" Gavin asked.

I told him what Tate told me. "I don't suppose Mom enlisted you to do it."

"No way. My parents would kill me if I was sneaking out every night this month. Besides, I never could keep a secret like that from you."

Kay took the mic and motioned to Amberlee. She gingerly walked up.

"Um. Hi. We'd...*I'd*...like to sh-sh-are a tra-a-a—" She took a deep breath. "We'd like to share a druid and a witch tradition. Winter solstice is special. And we acknowledge that tonight with all our friends and family. We ask you to join us in this ritual. Please. Step outside."

The guests rose and everyone followed her out.

I hadn't noticed it, but to the right of the house, was a large log wrapped in red ribbon and decorated in holly and evergreen boughs. I recognized herbs like rosemary and thyme, and they tucked feathers between the log and the cloth.

She stood before it, with a pine cone in her hand, and closed her eyes. "It is time to burn the Yule log."

Tate tugged on my arm. "Cool!"

We passed around a basket of pine cones. Each person took one.

"Take a moment to reflect on your life and your hopes and dreams. And the bad habits you wish to shed. Like the pinecone you hold in your hand, you also hold your life. It is your choice how you wish to use it."

That's one thing about Amberlee. When she feels secure and resolute, she never stumbles over words. She lit a torch using magic and touched it to the log. The flames shot up and seemed to sparkle like glitter as the wood crackled. The scent of the spices rose in the air and the burning wood snapped.

She handed the torch back to Kay and took the pine cone. She stood with her head bowed for a moment, then tossed it in. The flames changed colors from red to yellow with traces of blue. Smoke twined about her body and her hair floated as she seemed to glow from inside.

As each person took a turn, every one of the pine cones burned colors. Some only one color, some multiple.

Most of the people went inside, but some of us stayed to watch the flames. Gavin and I found a corner on the end of the porch. When I shivered, he pulled me close. "So, there's a shed in the back of the cottage. It'll be chilly, but we'll be alone—and I can keep you warm."

Gavin made me feel incredible. But while I stood, holding my pinecone, I thought about getting closer and everything in me whispered, "Wait."

"Like Mom says, 'I have plenty of time.'"

"What?" Gavin asked.

"Nothing. Let's go inside."

#

"That was lovely," Mom said to Kay and Amberlee.

Kay beamed. "Thank you for coming."

On our way back home, we saw footprints.

"Who would walk this way? The only place it leads to is our cottage," Mom said.

"After I get you home, I'll take a keek," Greg said.

Again, the footsteps led to our snowman. One of his boots had fallen off this time. Tate and I stayed outside to put him back together.

"Do you think Mr. Greg will find anyone?" Tate asked.

"I doubt it. Even if they were at the party, we were the last to leave, so they could have easily been here and gone in plenty of time."

"I just don't get it. Whoever it is just comes and walks around Frosty, then leaves? That's really weird." Tate rammed the snow-filled boot on top of Frosty's leg.

"Let's go inside. I'm cold. Maybe Mom will make cocoa."

Before I got to the door, I looked back, and I could have sworn I saw the snowman wink at me. With curiosity tugging at my feet, I jogged back to him and kneeled in the snow. His eyes were still regular walnuts, but I poked one to be sure. "I must have imagined it," I said as I went inside.

Chapter 6

Becca

I promised myself every year this year would be different. I'd be organized and get all my Christmas shopping done by November. And yet here it is, December 24th and I am in a mall furiously looking for last-minute gifts—again.

The entire family rode the ferry to the mainland, but once we disembarked, everyone took off in another direction like cats from a ferocious dog. Well, maybe not our cat, Tabby. She's a brave little girl.

I want this Christmas to be special—magical. It will be the first one we'll celebrate with Greg. He had been the most difficult to find a gift for.

I found a resale shop tucked in an out of the way spot, which made sense because it wasn't a big draw for the tourists.

The shop was busy, and the selection poor. All the better for my purpose.

"Can I help you? As you can see, we're pretty picked over, but if you'll tell me what you're looking for, I'll try to find it," a harried shop keeper offered.

"I'm not here to buy. I'm here to sell."

A smile broke out on the shopkeeper's face. "Follow me."

She led me to the vacant side of the cash register. The customers in line for purchases frowned until they saw I wasn't cutting to the front of the queue. She touched her nametag. "I'm Nancy."

"Becca. Nice to meet you."

"Let's see what you've got."

I smothered a sigh, and pulled the blouse out of the bag, the price tags still on it.

She took it, shook it out, and spread it on the countertop. "Oh, my! Are you sure you want to part with this?"

"I'm sure."

"You should take it back to the store you bought it from and return it. Is it the wrong size?"

"No, it fits, but it's from a boutique in the States. This is from their going-out-of-business sale." Earlier, I'd made a point of peeling the sales price off the tag. She didn't need to know what a good buy I got, and I was hoping to get more than what I paid.

Nancy carefully examined the blouse for flaws and stains. She found none, as I knew she would. She leaned close and whispered a price to me. I nodded.

"Great! The way it works is you get sixty percent of what we can sell it for and we keep forty percent."

I tried to do the math, but gave up and plugged the numbers in my phone. I smiled when I saw the result. "Wonderful. Do I get cash or a check?"

Nancy's face fell. "You get the money when we do, sweetie."

"You mean I have to wait until someone buys it?"

"Afraid so."

This was my last-ditch effort to get enough money for the gift that, after searching for the last two months, I'd found for Greg. "Okay, I understand. If I can't get the money now, it's no good to me." I picked up the blouse and the sack and turned to leave. As I did so, a hand darted out and grabbed the blouse sleeve.

"Whoa! Where did you find this and are there any more?" the woman said.

"Oh. I didn't buy it here. I was going to sell it but decided not to."

"Drats. But I don't blame you. The only time that blouse would leave my closet was when I was wearing it, if I owned it."

"You'd buy it?"

"How much?"

Nancy bustled out from behind the counter. "Hold on. She's selling the blouse to us. As soon as we complete the process, you can buy it."

"She's on her way out the door!" the shopper protested.

"You absolutely cannot buy items directly from the seller. That's not how it works," Nancy said firmly.

"What if we step outside?"

By now, everyone in the shop was staring at us.

Nancy also noticed everyone noticing us. "Look, I'm sure we can come to some sort of agreement," she said, to pacify the woman. I found myself being steered by my elbow to an office.

I didn't say anything and let Nancy and the shopper haggle. The only thing I stipulated was that I got sixty percent of the amount Nancy originally quoted to me. It took longer than I liked, and I was going to be hard pressed to get to my next destination before it closed, but they eventually came to numbers they could agree.

Nancy went to fetch my money as the woman fingered her new blouse.

"I know exactly where I'm wearing this."

"Oh?"

"My aunt is in poor health, so we're having a small family celebration at her home. It's been ages since I've visited, since I live in London, but I remember how posh it was. I'd hoped to find a little something impressive to wear, and this is perfect."

"I'm happy for you," I said.

After I signed the papers, Nancy handed me the money and I rushed out the door. The antique shop was sure to close promptly. It was Christmas Eve, after all.

#

The owner was just flipping the closed sign over when I barreled into him. "Whoa! I'd just about given up on you," he said.

I was very pleased with the gift I finally came upon for Greg, but it was expensive, and the antique owner had a hard time finding it.

He finished closing and locked the door. "I've already shut everything down, but we can still do business. Sit down. I'll bring it out."

I gingerly sat on a chair in one corner of the room. It was probably an antique, though not a rare one, since no one had roped off the seat. The shopkeeper came back with something square and wrapped in a cloth. He unwound the cloth to reveal a polished wooden box about twelve inches long, eight inches wide and six inches deep with decorative brass edgings. The clasp was also brass with a plate ornately decorated. Upon careful examination, I could just make out a scrolled, fancy letter "G." "Oh my! I never guessed you'd be able to find one with the correct initial," I said, admiring it.

"Neither did I, truth be told. You're one lucky lady."

"That I am."

He pulled out a drawer that was sectioned and contained a bristled shaving brush made of silver-tipped badger fur, a stainless-steel shaving bowl, a tube of paste, a tin of shaving soap, a leather strop, and one empty spot meant for a straight blade razor. "The paste is used to maintain the blade."

"Perfect. He'll love it."

"Someone came in earlier selling a razor. It'd fit in perfectly with this case. I can give you a special discount if you're interested."

"No. I'm good. But thanks."

Chapter 7

Tate

Do you have any more shopping to do?" Jessie asked.

"Nope. I just wanted to enjoy the street decorations one more time before they come down." We stopped to look in a store window displaying a fake Santa. He was reading a book, and beside him was a stack of Christmas themed books. I'd read most of them. "I may not know what I'm getting, but I know what everyone else is."

"I bet there's at least one person who you don't know what he's giving anyone."

"You're talking about Greg and you'd be wrong. I know what he's got you."

"I bet you don't know what he's getting Mom."

"I bet you don't either."

"You'd be wrong. I do." Jessie smugly grinned. "One upped you!"

"What did he get her?"

"I guess it won't hurt to tell you." Jessie sighed. "Let's go to the mall where we can sit down and warm up first."

We stopped by McD's for French fries and cokes, then took them to the food court to people watch while we ate.

"I can't believe they ran out of ketchup," Jess said.

"I bet I can find vinegar. I'll go ask at that place that serves fish and chips."

"Thanks."

"No stealing my French fries."

"Not happening. You're the fry thief."

She was right. I did sneak fries and always checked the emptied bag for strays. The counter man was happy to give me a handful of malt vinegar packets. As I returned, I snuck up behind Jess and stole a fry.

"Hey! Keep that up and you won't find out what Greg got Mom until tomorrow morning when she opens it."

"Come on. Don't tease."

"Okay, but don't you dare give it away to Mom. She's going to be thrilled."

"Well?"

"Greg needed my help with the gift. That's how I found out about it."

"What did he need you for?"

"He needed to know about what size Mom wears and what kind of skirts she likes."

"Mr. Greg is getting Mom clothes?"

"Not exactly. He wants to get Gillie tartan fabric for Mom to have a skirt made. He says the colors would look good with that fancy blouse Mom is always saying she'll wear, but never does because she has nothing that will match."

"Uh oh."

"What do you mean by that?"

"Mom's selling that blouse."

"Why? She loves it."

"She's selling it, so she has enough money to buy Mr. Greg a special antique shaving kit to go with his old-fashioned shaver."

"Oh, no."

"What?"

"Mr. Greg had to sell his shaver to have enough money to pay for the tartan."

"This is awful. We've got to do something."

"Maybe we can buy back the blouse and the razor. There can't be that many antique shops here. We can start calling and hopefully find the one he sold it to."

"It's a good thing we're already off the island. The cell phones work fine here and, since we're already here, we can run over and get it."

Jessie frantically searched her purse.

"What if the shopkeeper doesn't want to sell it?"

"He just has to!" She tossed her purse on the tabletop. "I forgot my phone! I left it set up in the kitchen to catch the elf mover and didn't pick it up on the way out!"

"We don't have much time. Let's go to the mall's information booth."

Chapter 8

Jessie

I was starving from running around all over the mainland looking for Greg's razor and Mom's blouse. The blouse was long gone. A woman in line snatched the blouse from Mom before the sales lady could even put a tag on it. The antique shop was closed, but we wrote a note and slipped it through the mail slot. It was late by the time we reached the ferry so, I promised to make dinner. It'd be faster and Mom usually did the washing up if I cooked. While Mom cleaned, I'd have time to wrap the presents.

I'd zoomed ahead of Mom and Tate, so I was the first person to see it. There was our snowman—but he was no longer standing on his head. "Mom!" I called back.

When she reached me and saw it, she gasped. "How... who....?"

"I don't know, but what a mean trick!"

Greg ran up. He must have seen us from the woods and could tell we were upset. "What's happened?"

"Somebody messed up our snowman!" Tate said.

Greg circled the snowman. "Dinna fash yourselves. He dinna appear damaged."

"No, but he's *supposed* to be upside down and it's going to be really hard to flip him," I pointed out. *Who would go to all the trouble to do this?*

"For now, we have plenty to do. We'll worry about it after Christmas."

"But Mo-om!" Tate and I said it to Mom in stereo.

We followed Mom inside.

"Really, girls. I need to make some calls about deliveries for Mrs. Nivens's Christmas. How are you coming with the ornaments?"

"We have a few more things we need to decorate that can dry overnight. Mr. Greg, do you want to help?" Tate asked.

"Aye, well, I'm nae good at art, but I can string more popcorn to decorate her tree."

"Jessie, check your phone!" Tate shouted.

Mom frowned. "What's wrong with your phone? Please tell me you didn't lose it."

"No Mom, but we set up a trap to see who's been moving the elf around. Tate overheard you and Mr. Greg discussing it."

"Tate Elizabeth." *Uh oh.* It's always a bad sign if Mom uses middle names.

"I wasn't snooping. I just heard something about the elf and got curious."

"Right. And that's why I found you looking through the closet yesterday?"

Tate blushed. "I wasn't looking for my presents. I was just curious about what you got everyone else."

"Oh, I'm sure that was the reason." She rolled her eyes. "Well, good luck, but I'll be surprised if you get anything on video. Is that why you two wanted to sleep in the living room last night?"

"We thought it was worth a try. We didn't tell you what we had in mind because we were afraid you'd tell whoever is moving the elf. You *do* know who's been doing it, right?"

"Yes, Greg and I stayed up one night and caught them in the act."

"Come on, Jessie. Let's see if you got anything."

I'd hidden the camera on the table facing the television. Tate and I left the television and kitchen light on, so it was dark enough to sleep, but light enough that hopefully, something would show up on the phone. The pose for the 23rd had Sir Clifford sitting on the television, fishing off the edge. We'd stayed up as late as we could. I set up the camera early, so I'd just have to start recording and if anyone was watching, they shouldn't notice.

I picked up the phone and checked the video. Tate crowded in beside me. Between the two of us, we stayed up until about four a.m. before I turned on the video. The elf had vanished and reappeared in the kitchen the following morning, but we had been running late and completely forgot to check the camera. At first, all we saw was the elf.

"Nothing's happening," Tate said, disappointment lowering her voice.

"Let's keep watching. We know Sir Clifford got moved, so something happened. Maybe they turned off the video, so all we'll see is a finger."

"Wait! Look in the corner." Tate pointed to a fuzzy part.

Then Sir Clifford took flight! I was afraid that all we would get to see is the elf being lifted, but after experimenting with the video, I was able to freeze a frame revealing a small creature with wings.

Tate gasped. "Is that a—"

"A pixie!" I exclaimed. "You guys let pixies move Sir Clifford around all this time?"

"By the time we finally caught them in action, there wasn't much time left before Christmas. I convinced Greg to let them keep doing it."

Greg grunted. "I wasna thrilled."

"And we didn't really catch them in the act. They found us asleep on the couch and played a trick that made Greg realize who they were."

"What did they do?" I asked.

Mr. Greg muttered something.

"What?"

"The wee pests braided my hair and your mother's!"

"You mean like they did to Grandma?"

"No, they only did one braid. I guess they didn't consider spying on the elf as bad as stealing," Mom said.

"I wonder why they didn't braid our hair?" Tate asked.

"Maybe they thought you two being curious was part and parcel of the job."

Mr. Greg cleared his throat and left the room.

Mom grinned. "Someday he's promised me he'll tell me why he dislikes pixies so much."

"Are you going to tell us, too?" Tate asked.

"I think I'll leave that up to Greg. After all, it's his story."

The antique store owner left a message on my phone. I hoped it was good news. I'd left a check for what Greg told me the tartan cost, hoping he'd accept it as payment. It was the largest one I had ever written, but I'd saved up quite a bit from working for Gavin's dad, Mr. Samms. Even if it was, I didn't see how we could get back to the mainland in time to fetch it.

We only had a few hours before we had to get ready for midnight mass. Since we stayed up the night before, it actually worked out well in preparation for a late night tonight.

#

After church, Mom said we could each open one gift. We'd probably unwrap the ones from Grandma. She usually recycled presents. Sometimes the gifts were from decades earlier. She followed suit this year. Mom got an awful crocheted doll you could hide a roll of toilet paper under. Tate got a book of paper dolls.

"Tate, be careful with those. I doubt if your grandmother knew it, but those may be worth something and, well, they're beautiful," Mom cautioned.

I wish I could say as much about the long skirt she got me. It was this awful orange that I'd only wear to a Halloween party. Reminded me of the color this one Oklahoma football team wore. Ick!

The funniest was Mr. Greg's. First, because she even got him one at all. And because she got him Old Spice! And it wasn't even the cologne.

"I dinna ken what you do with this," he said, as he took the top off and sniffed the protruding bar.

Mom frowned. "It's deodorant."

"Aye?"

Tate and I burst out laughing.

Mom recapped the deodorant and tossed it back in the bag. "I'll explain later."

Mom had been introducing Greg to Christmas movies, so we opened the huge tin of flavored popcorn Aunt Jan's family and our uncle got us. Though Mom says she'd be shocked if he really had contributed.

It didn't take long to decide which one we'd watch. It's funny. Even though it takes place during the Christmas season, we never considered *Die Hard* an actual Christmas movie until we moved to Scotland. We'll watch it this year and I think it'll become a new tradition. Greg should really like it. I mean, most guys do, since it's one of the few Christmas movies that isn't kind of syrupy sweet.

We always stayed up late on Christmas Eve. Mainly, I think, so Mom and Dad could sleep in, since they had to stay up after we went to bed and set out the toys. Dad used to grumble about batteries and poorly worded instructions. So, we had time for two movies. This year we'd watch John McClane fight baddies in a tower. Then we'd watch an old black and white favorite, *It's a Wonderful Life*.

As Tate passed around bowls of popcorn, I watched my mom and Greg. He'd wrapped his arm around her shoulder and she leaned into him, chuckling at something he'd said. Since Mom met Greg, she'd been less tense. She laughed more often. Greg had chilled out, too. He never would have played tricks on Tate and me even a few months ago. I really miss Dad, but Mom and Greg were good for each other, and I loved seeing my mom smile again.

Chapter 9
Greg

The tartan came yesterday, just in the nick of time. The money I got for the razor was barely enough. It was a good thing Kay didna have the time to sew the skirt before Christmas, because I couldna have afforded to pay for it if she had.

Last night, the snow came down in droves and the temperature dropped. I wasna sure the ferry would be sailing until the weather warmed. Before I went to Rebecca's cottage, I'd take a walk around and check on the neighbors. I knew she wanted to go to Mrs. Nivens to drop off Christmas decorations before it got too late. So, everything would be up before her relatives arrived. If they didna miss the ferry.

As I traveled around, I also checked for signs of the fae. I was hoping for a quiet day so I could spend all of it with my family. *My family.* I nae thought I'd be lucky enough to say that again. After I lost my expectant wife and bairn, I thought my life was over. I never dreamed I'd find love. Here I am, dating a wonderful woman and spending time with her two equally wonderful daughters. Ice hung from the trees and sparkled in the sun. My breath puffed out before me. The pond was frozen over for the first time in decades. I dinna see the weeping lady. Being part fae though, I was sure she was okay. Snow was piled high, but thanks to my Keeper ability to travel with ease through the forest, it nae slowed me down.

Mr. Samms was already out with his plow, clearing the roads. He waved at me. "Happy Christmas!" he called.

"Happy Christmas to you too," I replied.

"I'll see you at Mrs. Nivens's after I clear the road."

"Aye."

"Since my oldest boy and his fellow band members are stuck on the island, I'm going to put them to work. They just got back from the pier. The ferry's not going anywhere, so I have extra guests for Christmas."

I checked on McVitie, the selkie, first. He was outside mending nets in his shirt sleeves. The man must be part polar bear. The cold nae bothers him at all.

"Ferry's nae running," he gruffly informed me.

"Mr. Samms mentioned it. Weather's bad out on the water?"

"Aye." Mr. McVitie was a man of few words.

"Are you going to Mrs. Nivens?"

"Aye. I'm bringing smoked salmon."

"That's verra generous." I'd had McVitie's smoked salmon before and hadna tasted any better.

"Think Mrs. Nivens's kin made it?"

I shrugged. "If not, she'll still have plenty of people to celebrate with her."

#

After I finished my rounds and found all well, I hied to the cottage. When I arrived, Jessie was putting the finishing touches on another batch of gingerbread men. "Ready to go?" I asked.

Rebecca nodded. "I spoke to Kay on the phone. Amberlee and she had planned to go to the mainland to spend Christmas with Amberlee's family, but they're stuck here."

"Aye. The ferry barely made it back from the mainland. It isna going out until the weather warms."

"I told Kay they were welcome to come over here for Christmas. They purposely skimped on groceries because they knew they'd be gone."

"Are the girls champing at the bit to open their gifts?"

"Not Jess. She knows what her presents are. Tate's curious. Thankfully, getting everything ready to go to Mrs. Nivens curbed her nosiness. Oh, and Kay offered to pick us up. Hope that's okay. It might be a tight fit, so I may end up having to sit on your lap." She blinked up at me.

"Aye? I dinna have a problem with that." I stole a kiss.

"Ugh. Stop the kissy-facing!" Jess said.

"There's no way all this is going to fit in Kay's car along with whatever she's bringing too."

A phone rang. All four of us checked ours.

"It's mine," Jess said.

"Gavin?" I guessed. Since she hied to the bedroom.

Rebecca threw her arms up and rolled her eyes. "That's young love for you."

"I saw Mr. Samms. All the band members are stuck on the island, as well."

"Wow. That's five extra hungry young people, if Mr. Samms's son was planning to leave with them," Rebecca said.

Jessie returned. "Gavin says that his dad is going to drive the tractor around the neighborhood. If anyone needs a ride, we need to let him know."

"How do you girls feel about riding the tractor? Warning, you'll also be in charge of the items we're bringing over."

"Cool. Gavin said his dad had already dropped off his mom, his brother and the other band members. I wonder if they'll play for Mrs. Nivens. After they set up the tree, they'll help load and unload the wagon."

Jessie called her young laddie back to set things up. After we got everything out to the wagon and strapped it all down, Kay drove us to Mrs. Nivens.

Once on the big house's door stoop, I lifted the wolf's head knocker and let it drop three times. Dorcas tugged open the door. Noting our filled arms, she said, "Oh my! This is so much more than I expected."

"How's Mrs. Nivens reacted to all the visitors and goodies?" Rebecca asked.

"She's getting up a bit later these days. Oh, my goodness, she's going to be so surprised," Dorcus gushed with pink tinted cheeks. "Hopefully, once the others arrive, we can get the tree and house decorated before she comes down. Mrs. Samms came early this morning and put a turkey and ham in the oven."

"Where do you want these?" Rebecca asked, holding out a box filled with Kay's homemade decorations.

"Take any ornaments to the table by the tree. The food goes in the kitchen." Dorcas pointed as she bustled off, but then stopped, turned, and said, "Happy Christmas and bless you!" Kay and Amberlee followed her.

"I'm sure they don't want me anywhere near the cooking," Rebecca said to me. I knew better than to agree, so I clamped my lips together and followed her to the tree.

A man I dinna ken came in carrying firewood. "Hello, ma'am." From her look of confusion, Rebecca dinna ken him at first, either.

"Don't recognize me off the boat, do you?" he asked.

Recognition dawned on Rebecca's face. "Oh! It's the ferry operator, Greg." She turned to him. "No, I didn't. Merry Christmas!"

"I have something for your girls. Are they here yet?"

"No. They're riding over with Mr. Samms."

He nodded. "Not having a car on the island usually isn't a big deal, but with this weather—brr! I'm thankful the kind doctor gave me a ride tonight. But enough chitchat, I'd better get these fires going."

"That's odd. I wonder what in the world the ferry operator wanted with my daughters?" Rebecca asked.

I climbed the ladder to decorate the top portion of the tree. The blue-green hued noble fir was great in size, but a bit shabby on one side. We turned it so only the pretty full branches faced the center of the room.

"It's a pity no one thought to bring lights for the trees," Rebecca commented, handing me an ornament.

The Samms's family brought two trees, one for the entryway and one for the parlor. Lundy arrived with an armload of mistletoe and holly. As Mr. Samms returned, he honked the horn, beckoning people to come help him with unloading.

A man came inside carrying a box of Christmas crackers. "Hello," he said. At my confused look, he smiled. "Don't have any more complaints about my selection of plaids, do you? Happy Christmas, Greg Gillie."

It was that bampot of a bloke from the tartan store. I dinna expect to see him here. "Happy Christmas," I parroted back at him.

Tate and Jessie came bearing more ornaments. Rebecca divvied them up and sent the girls with half to fill in the other tree.

With everyone working together, the decorations were up and sparkling like precious stones by the time Mrs. Nivens came down the stairs. "Dorcas, what on earth is this?!"

Calls of "Happy Christmas" rang out.

"This was all wee Tate's idea," Dorcas said.

Someone must have fetched Tate from the parlor. "Merry Christmas, Mrs. Nivens!" She gave her a hug and I could see the shine of happy tears in Mrs. Nivens's eyes.

Then Dorcas ushered a small group of people inside. I dinna have room to put any more ornaments on the tree, so I climbed down the ladder and joined Rebecca.

"That must be Mrs. Nivens's relatives. I recognize her sister," she said.

An elderly lady gawked at the crowd of people and the lavish room filled with decorations. "Sissy! What on earth?"

Mrs. Nivens preened. "Happy Christmas, dear. Since you'd said the family could only stay for a few hours, I opened my house to the islanders. I'm sure you won't mind."

The younger woman said, "Actually, we're snowed in, Aunt Mornia."

Rebecca looked like she'd seen a ghost.

"Do you ken her?" I asked.

"Yes. I saw her on the mainland."

"Small world."

Chapter 10

Becca

"Greg, why don't you go see if they need any help in the kitchen?"

"I dinna think they want nor need me there. What would I do?"

"They might need help carving the turkey. Or getting it out of the oven."

"You ken they got it *in* the oven just fine, right?"

"Please."

Greg left just as Tate joined me. "Are we really going to stay?"

"I suppose we should. I've been by the kitchen and from the wonderful aromas, we'd be eating better here than at home. We can always open gifts later."

Mrs. Nivens's niece shrugged off her coat.

"Mom, she's wearing your blouse!" Tate said, loud enough to turn heads.

"Shh!"

"And it doesn't fit her."

"Tate, it doesn't matter. I sold it to her. It's hers now." The woman's eyes widened as she recognized me. I waved and forced a smile on my face.

"I gotta find Jess," Tate said, and scampered off.

I looked out the window. The snow was falling harder. I couldn't see Kay's car or the Samms' wagon, even though they were parked only a few yards away from the house.

"Hi Becca." Amberlee had joined me by the window. "Looks like we're going to be guests for a while longer. We probably won't be able to leave until Mr. Samms takes the plow through again." She sighed. I felt for her. As shy as Amberlee was, I knew she preferred the more intimate setting of our cottage.

Tate and Jessie approached Mrs. Nivens's niece and urgently spoke to her. They followed her upstairs, helping her carry bags. "What are those two up to?"

"What?" Amberlee asked.

"I think my daughters are up to something."

"But isn't it that way during the holidays?" Amberlee asked.

"You have a point."

The storm darkened the sky. Dorcas and Mr. McVitie lit the many candles sitting out. "If you're willing, we can give them a little help with the lighting for the trees," Amberlee commented.

"What do you mean?"

"Do you remember the light spell I taught you?"

"Yes." *Well, kind of.*

"If we pool our powers, we should be able to light the Christmas trees."

I chuckled. "You've better wait on Jessie for that."

"I'll wait for her, but your only problem is confidence, Becca. You need to believe in yourself."

Jessie came downstairs carrying a bag.

"What do you have?" I asked.

"Nothing." She set it beside her purse that was hanging on the hall tree.

I rolled my eyes at Amberlee, who then explained her plan.

"Won't the people visiting figure it out?"

"They're upstairs. If we do it quickly, by the time they come down, the trees will be lit. And—"

"Even if they look, they'll believe they're just a new kind of light."

We lit the two Christmas trees with whispered spells. The trees softly glowed as if covered in tiny fireflies, drawing attention to the beautiful decorations.

Mrs. Samms came to the hallway. "Hello? Can I have your attention?"

Everyone paused. "Dinner will be ready at two."

There were some groans.

"To take your minds off your bellies, the Thistle Throstles have agreed to play music. If I can get some men to help clear the floor, we can have some dancing room."

Mrs. Samms got a round of applause. "I'll also be putting out appetizers. Help yourself to whatever's out. Just stay out of the kitchen!" she warned.

I helped carry trays of cheese cubes, tiny salmon sandwiches, and meatballs with stacks of paper plates and napkins.

The band set up in one corner of the great hall and tuned their instruments. Mr. Samms passed by, bundled up in his coat. "You aren't going out in that, are you?" I asked.

"I know this island like the back of my hand. It will be easier to plow a few times during the day instead of waiting until there's a great pile to do all at once. Gavin's going with me, and if it's okay, Jess would like to go, too."

"I don't know. Are you sure it's safe?"

"It is. Gavin's gone out with me many a time."

"Then it's okay with me."

Jess and Gavin followed. Jessie had found an oversized snowsuit she wore over her jeans. She'd rolled up the sleeves and legs.

"Are you sure you want to go out in this?"

"Yeah. It won't take long and Mrs. Samms wants us to pick up a couple of things."

I noticed Jess had the bag but said nothing. Maybe it was something for Tate. Speaking of which — "Do you know where your sister is?"

"She's in the kitchen."

By the time Mr. Samms returned, his wife had the grand buffet ready to go, and the hungry guests loaded their plates, then scurried to various rooms to grab a drink and eat. After we filled our tummies with Mrs. Samms's delightful food, we gathered in the parlor with our hostess. The teens passed out glasses of champagne to the adults while they drank sparkling grape juice.

"Before we have dessert, let's raise a glass to Mrs. Nivens, our host." Mrs. Samms lifted her glass toward Mrs. Nivens. "Thank you for sharing your home on this blessed holiday, Mrs. Nivens. This gathering shall go down in the Shrouded Isle history as the best Christmas ceilidh ever!"

Mrs. Nivens's sister helped her rise. "I know it was an especially happy Christmas ceilidh for me. I want to thank all of you." Mrs. Nivens's chin wobbled, and she checked her pockets for a tissue.

Greg came to the rescue and presented her with his handkerchief. "If you didna ken how much we care about you, you should now, Mrs. Nivens. You're an important part of the Shrouded Isle."

"Ho, ho, ho!" A man in a red suit trimmed with white fur and black boots stomped in through the front door. A long white beard and wavy white hair obscured his face.

"It's Santa!" a child cried out.

"Happy Christmas," the man shouted.

Mrs. Nivens's nephew, Conall, brought him one of the dining room chairs. He unslung a large brown bag from his back. "Thank you for coming," Conall said, solemnly, obviously in on it.

"I wouldn't miss this party for the world!" the man said, then laughed again, holding his belly.

I grabbed Kay's sleeve. "Who is it?"

"I don't know. Conall must have set it up."

"I have gifts for everyone!" Santa called out.

The children squealed with excitement.

Conall and Lundy chivvied them into a line of sorts. Santa handed out a small gift and a candy cane to each child.

When he finished, he looked around. "Now surely those weren't the only ones good this year?"

Conall beamed. "Mrs. Nivens, you first."

To her surprise, Santa insisted she sit on his lap.

"Are you sure your lap can take it?" she asked, grinning mischievously.

"Aye. You're as pretty as a picture and as light as a song," Santa replied.

"Is that a blush on Mrs. Nivens's face?" Greg whispered.

"I believe so. This Santa is quite the charmer."

Instead of reaching into the large bag, Santa tugged a small jewelry box from his jacket pocket. "Sometimes the best treasures are the ones we lost long ago," Santa said in a soft voice. He opened the case.

Mrs. Nivens gasped. "It can't be!"

"But it is." He drew a brooch shaped like a thistle from the case. "May I?" he asked her. She nodded. He pinned it on the lapel of her dress.

"But I lost this years ago. My husband got me this brooch for my birthday. See the jewels? The purple are amethysts for February, the month I was born and the green are emeralds for May, his month. I wore it for years. The clasp came undone when I was on the ferry and it fell into the water."

"The clasp is fixed, so you'll never lose it again."

She fingered the brooch. "How in the world did you find it? I thought I'd never see it."

"It was found caught up in kelp."

"What a wonderful Christmas gift!" She threw her arms around Santa and hugged him.

Conall took her hand and helped her off Santa's lap. Mrs. Nivens joined her family to show them the gift.

Santa turned to the rest of us. "There are after-dinner drinks for the adults. Mrs. Samms has the desserts ready in the dining room. Hurry along! You'll not want to miss the lighting of the Christmas pudding!"

I wasn't a big fan of Christmas pudding, so I held Greg back while we let others go in ahead of us.

Greg tilted his head toward Santa, who was gathering his bag. I took his hand, and we joined the jolly man.

"I don't suppose you'll be Santa every year," I said, still unsure who I addressed.

"Nae. I usually keep to myself."

"I'm glad you didn't this year."

Dorcas joined us. "Um, Santa? The coast is clear. We can sneak you up the back stairs."

"Happy Christmas, Greg and Becca." He followed Dorcas to the door, but before he went through, he turned and tugged his beard down only for a sec. But it was long enough for us to recognize who Santa was.

"I'd nae thought of such happening," Greg said, shaking his head.

I thought about what Mrs. Nivens had said about the brooch. "Do you think that Mr. McVitie found the brooch in the water during one of his swims?" Mr. McVitie was a male selkie.

"It wouldna surprise me."

A snowball splatted against the window. "The snow must have stopped," I commented as I peeked out the window at the crystal-clear sky and the cottony snowdrifts. "What a cute idea." Someone had made a giant sign saying "Merry Christmas and Happy New Year" by stomping the letters in the snow. Beside the message stood a snowman.

I grabbed Greg's sleeve. "Wait a minute. Is that—"

Greg nodded. "Aye, that's the girls' Frosty. Let's get to the bottom of this."

As we marched to the door, Amberlee stopped us. "What's wrong? Why are you so serious-looking?"

"Something magical is happening, and it isna the fae," Greg said. "We're investigating."

"I'll go with you. I can tell if it's witch work."

On our path to the outside, we gained three more followers: Kay and the two girls.

Greg threw open the door and gestured at the lawn. "See?"

"It's a nice sentiment," Kay commented. "But I don't see why the changelings would do something like this. They'd be more likely to destroy the snowman and Christmas decorations."

Amberlee rubbed her arms, stepped out onto the lawn and studied not the message, but the snowman. Then she laughed. "I think I know exactly what's happened. Jessie? Do you want to explain?"

"But I didn't do anything," Jess protested, then noticed Frosty. "Hey! That's our snowman!"

"And you've put a spell on him, haven't you?" Amberlee asked.

"Well, yes. We didn't want him to melt. So, I looked through the spell book to see if there was anything I could do to prevent it. It worked. He's the same size as when we first made him."

"Do you remember when I told you how important intent was when doing a spell?" Amberlee asked.

Jessie nodded. "Yes."

"Your spell did more than make him impervious to the heat. You've infused him with life."

Greg hit his thigh with his fist. "So that's the creature everyone has been seeing!" He turned to the rest. "I've been seeing something white in the forest. Other villagers also said they had too, but no one had gotten close enough to tell exactly what it was."

"Our snowman has been walking around?" Tate asked.

"Aye. Mostly at night and I guess always when everyone in the house was gone or asleep," he answered. "At least that's one mystery solved. But he canna stay alive and running around forever."

"And he won't. A spell like this has a time limit," Amberlee said.

"How long *will* he last?" Tate asked.

"I'm guessing by January, he'll stop moving and will start melting," Amberlee answered.

"No harm done, but Jessie, you may want to run any new spells past Amberlee. We're lucky an army of gingerbread men didn't descend upon us."

"I guess Frosty has made all the footprints we've been seeing whenever he left and came back to the cottage," Jessie said.

This made me feel better. "At least we know that no one has sneaked up to our cottage and snooped around."

"Yeah, that's great news. It also means that the changelings have been quiet so far—which is even better news," Kay said.

"Yes, but I don't think it will last."

"Nor do I, but it's a blessing for the holidays, to be sure."

"Do you think the snowman will return home?" I asked.

Amberlee nodded. "I'm guessing he'll be there by the time you get home."

"Wow, Jess. That spell was even cooler than we thought it was," Tate enthused.

I stared thoughtfully at Jessie. "She really is going to be very powerful, won't she?" I whispered to Amberlee.

Amberlee patted my hand. "Don't worry, Becca. She's a good girl. I won't say that she will make no mistakes along the way to becoming a masterful witch, but she's a loving young lady and anything she gets wrong, she'll correct it."

Kay chuckled. "Always with the worrying."

I chuffed. "I think that is part and parcel of being a Keeper and a parent, unfortunately."

Amberlee touched my hand. "Maybe someday, the one who gave the two of you that duty will take it away for good."

"That would be like a dream come true, but what would it mean for the fae?" I asked.

"And for us?" Greg added.

Kay grinned. "It would mean that you'd have your lives to yourselves. If you wanted to move, say, back to the States, then you could. It would open up many avenues to the two of you."

Greg shook his head. "It's a pleasant dream, but only a dream. I canna see it ever happening."

"I bet you never saw Becca coming here, either. And you and she caring for one another? And her staying here to help you with your duty? Did you?" Kay said.

"Nae. Tis true. I guess, really, anything is possible."

"And thank goodness for that."

"Let's go inside before I freeze!" Tate said, then she picked up snow, made a ball and pelted her sister.

As she ran, Jessie yelled, "Just you wait! You are so going to get it," and took off after her.

"Oh, to be young," Kay said.

Amberlee took her hand. "I don't know. I'm quite happy with the stage I'm at right now." The two followed the girls inside.

Greg looked down at me with a gleam in his eye. "Aye. I'm quite happy with my stage and my life, too."

Exaggerating it, I looked around. "Greg, don't look now, but we're alone!" I whispered.

"Aye, that we are." He also examined the area, then swept me up in his arms and kissed me until I didn't even notice the cold.

Chapter 11

Becca

We got home shortly before dinner. Though we brought home leftovers from the party, I doubted anyone would be hungry enough to eat. Then again, there was sticky toffee pudding, Greg's favorite.

The girls' aunt left several messages. I called her back, and we both put our phones on speaker so everyone could hear and take part in the conversation. The first thing Jessie and Tate's grandmother did was complain we hadn't been available in the morning to talk. The girls told them about Mrs. Nivens and what everyone did to make the older woman's holiday special. "Oh Grandma, the surprise ceilidh was just amazing! You should have seen all the people, the lights, and the look on Mrs. Nivens's face." Of course, the girls had to explain that a ceilidh was just a Scottish word for a party.

After I hung up, Tate said, "We've never opened gifts this late. Who's going to be Santa?"

"Why don't we let Greg?" I suggested.

"I hope I dinna need to come down the chimney," he said.

I grinned. "No. It just means you hand out the gifts."

He rubbed his hands together, blowing a breath into his palms. "First, I'm lighting the fireplace, though."

While he prepared the fireplace, I poured the eggnog Kay sent back with us. I added a sprinkle of nutmeg and a generous amount of whisky. Then I made hot cocoa with marshmallows and chocolate chips for the girls.

In short order, we curled up on the floor in front of the blaze. I shut my eyes for a moment, taking in the cozy feel of the fire warming my family as the moment warmed my heart.

"Aye. Who should I start with?" Greg asked.

"Start with Tate," Jessie said.

Greg handed her the gift.

"That's from me," Jess said.

"Let her read the tag, Jess." I had no idea what the girls had gotten. Tate would give something artsy. I had no clue about Jess, though.

Tate wasted no time ripping through the paper. "Wow."

"What is it?"

She held up a box. "It's a 3D pen!" She turned to her sister and hugged her.

"Wow, Jess. You've outdone yourself. I hope you didn't spend that much on me."

Jessie grinned. "Tate and I pooled our money to get your gift and Greg's."

"And you'll love them!" Tate enthused.

Greg and I opened a few presents. Kay had knitted a green scarf for Greg and a gold sweater for me. I immediately slipped mine over my blouse. Amberlee made sachets from dried flowers and herbs. For Greg, she made herbal tea.

The girls opened the rest of their gifts in record time. Greg handed his gifts to the girls. He had taken a page out of Tate's book and his presents to them were handmade. He'd carefully carved out the girls' names. The wood gleamed, and the letters were beautiful. The girls seemed to love them and we had to wait as they ran back to their room to choose places to display them.

They thanked him enthusiastically when they came back, much to my delight. I looked around the Christmas tree and only saw a few more gifts to unwrap. I didn't know what the girls got me and Greg, nor what Greg had for me and was beyond curious. There were only the gifts for Greg and I from the girls, and the two gifts Greg and I gave each other.

"Shall we open your gifts?" I asked the girls. They shook their heads.

"We want to see what you got each other," Jessie said. Tate winked at me, so I guess she kept it to herself what I'd gotten Greg. Greg handed me possibly the worst wrapped present I'd ever seen.

"I didna ken how to do it."

I took the mistletoe bow off the top. "It's lovely." I really wanted to put the gift down and just watch him open mine, and I suspect he wished the same. He'd wrapped the paper around several times, but eventually I removed it all. My box was large and on the heavy side. He refused to open his box and waited for me.

"Please," he said.

I lifted the lid. Inside, nestled in the tissue paper, was a beautiful tartan of blue, gold and cream with thin lines of two other colors running through it.

"See the green?" Greg pointed. "It'll be bonny with that blouse."

My face fell. How was I going to tell him I'd sold my blouse? Before I could open my mouth, Jessie said, "Mr. Greg, you've got to open your gift next!"

He lifted the wooden box from the paper. "Fine craftsmanship. The man who carved this ken what he was about."

"Look inside," I said.

He flipped open the lid and stared.

"Do you know what it is?" I asked. His expression worried me. Did the antiques seller steer me to something that was too old or too new for Greg to recognize his present?

"Aye. I ken. It's a fine shaving kit. One of the finest I've seen."

Before he could say another word, Jessie plunked a gift on my lap. "This is from me and Tate," she said.

Tate handed Greg a small box. "Here's our gift to you, Mr. Greg."

We slowly opened our gifts. Possibly more slowly than we had opened the ones from each other.

I gasped when I saw mine. "My blouse! How did you—"

"My razor," Greg cried out.

The girls beamed.

"Mr. Greg asked me to help him get the tartan for you, Mom. So, I knew he'd sold his razor," Jess said.

"And you told me about the shaving kit, so I knew about the blouse," Tate said.

"I guess I'm very lucky I have two daughters who are so close that they share secrets," I said.

Greg placed the razor back in the box. "I canna accept this. This is too expensive a gift."

"Oh yes, you will!" Jessie said. "A lot of people went to a lot of trouble to get that." She told us about her phone call to the antiques dealer and how he didn't get her message until after we'd left for home. "He ran to the ferry and convinced the operator to take it back with him."

Worried, I gazed at my youngest. "Tate, please don't tell me you stole this blouse from Mrs. Nivens' niece."

"You saw how it was a bit too small and gaped in the front? I asked her about it and she said she loved it, but she'd have to convince the consignment shop to take it back. Jess and I had given up on ever seeing it again, so we bought another blouse for you. It wasn't the same, but it was the best we could do. She agreed to trade blouses if we paid the difference."

I couldn't believe the girls had been so attentive. I was especially over the moon that they thought of Greg. It's Christmas, and though I like to think of the girls as being thoughtful, most kids can't resist the what-am-I-getting siren call that the holiday played endlessly during TV commercials. The one that makes a person think of what they would get, rather than about what to get others. We encourage it in a way. After all, don't we have children write Christmas lists to Santa each year? And what happens to those lists? Parents use them to shop for their kids. And of course, the children figure this out very early in life.

"That was so sweet of the two of you, but this blouse, even on sale, was very expensive."

Tate beamed. "You and Mr. Greg are worth it, Mom."

Like Mrs. Nivens, my eyes filled with happy tears. I clasped my daughters close and Greg enveloped the three of us in a hug.

Our first Christmas together with Greg on the Shrouded Isle was more perfect and magical than I could ever have imagined. I have two of the most amazing children ever and, after grieving so long, Greg and I found each other. If the rest of our lives together are as wonderful as today, then we are a truly blessed family.

The End

I hope you had fun on your holiday visit to the Shrouded Isle and you've enjoyed the tale as much as I enjoyed researching and writing it. Thanks for reading and please consider writing a review. I'm grateful for all feedback.

Continue reading for a sneak peek of books 1 and 2 of the series

And a bonus short story, SPRING SHENANIGANS

KILTS AND CATNIP
Shrouded Isle, Scotland

"Mom, Mom, wake up!"

I lifted my head as my eldest's finger jabbed me in the rib three times in rapid succession. *Teen must maintain minimum touching to avoid icky mommy cooties, no doubt.* Despite lack of sleep, my inner monologue continued to function well. The dim night-light from the hall glowed bright enough to reveal Jessie standing beside the bed.

"What?" I rubbed my dry, gritty eyes and winced at the soreness. Late yesterday evening, we arrived at the summer cottage after a grueling drive and a vomit-inducing ferry trip. When the bags still weren't unpacked by eleven, I opted to go to bed and deal with it tomorrow. *Hello, tomorrow.*

"Tate's gone."

As I swung my legs over to sit up, Jessie stepped back. Her gaze alternated between me and the bedroom the girls shared next to mine. Jessie hugged her chest and fidgeted in that gawky, yet attractive way only fifteen-year-old girls can.

I shook my head. "What do you mean she's gone?" I squinted at the clock, but I had neglected to reset it to the correct time. A glance out the window revealed the star-filled sky. "Jess! It's the middle of the night! What the—" I said, barely checking myself before I blurted out a profanity. "Did you check the couch? She probably snuck out to read and fell asleep." I glanced at my pillow with longing.

Jessie's nails bit into my forearm and drove the sleep from my mind. My cool, unconcerned teen looked panicked. "I saw a boy take Tate into the woods. We gotta go now or we'll lose her!" she cried.

Fear drew an icy finger down my spine. Jessie tugged at me. Her eyes opened wide, large, like an anime character's.

"Tate? Tate, honey, where are you?" I received no answer. I shoved my feet into wellies and threw on my green, corduroy jacket I'd left on a chair. Jessie dragged me toward the door, but suspicious, I pulled free. "What *exactly* did you see? And I swear, if this is some kind of prank, you and your sister cooked up—"

"No prank."

"Then what?"

Jessie ran to the living room. "Come on!"

I followed, glanced at the girls' empty beds in the next room as I passed, then turned up the gas lamp, and blinked owlishly.

"I heard shuffling noises. I looked up and the window was open wide."

I drew close and squeezed her shoulder. "We left the window open, honey."

"Not wide open, Mom. We left it cracked this much." She held up her hands, showing a four-inch gap between them. "I went to lower it and saw a little boy dragging Tate into the woods. Tate was moving slowly, like she was sleepwalking."

I opened the front door and switched on the porch light. The girls' room was on the right side of the small house. I rushed around the corner in time to see a bluish light illuminate two figures, one in a nightgown and the other so much into the shadows that I couldn't make out any detail. They disappeared into the foliage. I knew the ruffled, pink pajamas. They were Tate's favorite. *What was she thinking?* She's old enough to know better than to wander off with a stranger.

Despite wanting to rush after her, I paused. *Bad idea to go into a forest, especially in the dark, Becca.* I remembered seeing a large flashlight on top of the refrigerator. Ignoring my warning, I raced back into the kitchen and rose on tiptoe to reach the light, so I could follow.

Jessie gripped my arm. "I'm coming too," she pleaded.

"Jess, if I hurry, I should be able to get her before I get completely turned around. I need you to stay here and call nine-nine-nine, in case I can't find her." Jessie opened her mouth ready to protest. Before she could speak, I added, "My cell is in my purse on the table." Then I remembered the friendly local we'd met when we first arrived. "Better yet, call Mr. McNeil from the grocery. His number is in my contacts, and he's sure to know who best to call."

Jessie rushed to the table for the phone.

Yelling Tate's name, I ran into the night and dashed toward the forest, thanking God the boy hadn't taken her to the ocean side of the cottage and carried my baby away in a boat. The forest felt too quiet as I dodged around an enormous oak. I ran until my boot heel caught on a root and made me stumble on the uneven ground. Frantic, I swung the light back and forth searching for my youngest. How could they have gotten so far ahead of me?

"Tate!" I called.

Scuffing my feet and tearing at bushes, I hoped to mark my path so we could find our way back or at least *be* found. The branch on a log snagged my clothes, and I fell to my knees.

Come on, Becca. Stop panicking. I stood, flipping off the flashlight. After listening for a few seconds, I heard rustling ahead to the north. Once more, though much dimmer, the blue light flickered ahead. I was afraid to switch on my light because it dimmed the indistinct blue. The eerie glow grew fainter. I kept calling and blundered forward, crying out as the light vanished.

"Tate!" I screamed, pausing to turn on the light. I spun, lighting up the dark earth around me. *My baby's gone.* I realized my mistake after making one full circle. I'd forgotten which direction I was going and where I'd come from. My heart beat a tattoo on my ribs, and I fought the primal urge to run—to find her. Find her now! But ingrained knowledge stilled my feet. I had to stop. I'd only injure myself rushing around in the dark, and I couldn't risk it. My girls needed me. Sinking to the ground, I rested my back against a tree. My breath came in gasps. I didn't want to just sit here, but when lost in the woods, the best thing you could do was stay put—and I was very lost. I choked back a sob, hoping in the silence, I would hear them. No telling how long I would be stranded in the forest and, when the searchers arrived, they would call my name, so I turned off the flashlight, conserving the battery. My head spun and I took deep breaths, trying not to hyperventilate. I forced myself to close my eyes and stop searching the night for the bobbing blue light that had long since vanished.

I didn't know how much time passed when I heard a twig snap. If it was an animal, I doubted I was in any danger, but I turned on the light, all the same, blinking as my pupils adjusted. Could Tate have gotten away? Was she making her way back to me? I shined the light into the darkness toward the noise. A hand brushed aside a large tree limb, revealing a dark-haired man in a kilt holding my daughter. As he stepped forward, he released the limb and it sprang back into place and quivered.

"Could you not shine that in my eyes?" he called out, squinting.

I kept the torch on but pointed it toward the ground as I struggled to my feet.

Glassy-eyed, Tate yawned. "Mama?"

I held out my arms. "Sweetie."

One moment, the man stood yards away—the next, the stranger deposited my daughter into my embrace then retreated. I gasped, hugging her close. The flashlight bobbed as I juggled it and Tate. I focused the light ahead. Starlight gleamed off the shoulder-length, wavy, black hair of a man paused in motion. I panned the light down, revealing a broad back clad in a white tunic. The hem of a green and blue kilt swung against his legs. He glanced over his shoulder at me and squinted once more. A look of surprise crossed his face.

As he stared, he turned and took a step closer. "It canna be," he whispered, as his harsh, stern features softened in wonder. He regarded me for a moment then frowned and shook his head.

"What were you doing with my daughter?" I demanded.

His lip curled. "Saving her from a worse fate than having a neglectful mum."

"She was sleeping! Someone took her from her bedroom. Was it you?" I sputtered. Jessie said it was a little boy, but maybe she was mistaken.

He ignored my question. "I would thank you kindly to leave my forest," he said, his countenance stern and his green eyes narrowing. A thick lock of raven-colored hair hung down, almost covering his left eye. His expression warmed when he looked at Tate, but his voice remained gruff. Before he turned and disappeared, he added, "And dinna come back."

Tate mewled like a kitten, very unlike her usual bawl.

"Hey, wait! Where are you going?" I yelled. I cast my light in his direction, but only saw him for a moment before the forest swallowed him. I couldn't believe he'd left us alone. I patted Tate. "Someone will find us. Try not to worry." She nuzzled my neck and sobbed. Ahead, an orange light flickered. "What in the world—"

I recognized a blaze in the distance and used the flashlight to weave around trees and over bushes to the edge zof the forest. When I stepped out, I heard a cry. Jessie ran to me, nearly bowling me over.

"Mrs. Shaw? Are you and the wee one all right?" Mr. McNeil, the grocer, called from the fire pit.

The man bore a striking resemblance to the ranger who traveled with a dwarf and an elf in that fantasy movie the girls loved. His tangled, dark hair fell an inch short of brushing his shoulders. I decided he must be one of those men who could grow a beard practically overnight because he looked as if a couple of days had passed without a razor touching his ruggedly handsome face. As he drew closer, I saw he wore unlaced hiking boots, creased jeans, and a white sleeveless undershirt which revealed tanned, toned arms.

"We're fine, Mr. McNeil. Thank you so much for coming."

Tate was getting heavy, so I put her down and led the two girls back to the house. Mr. McNeil followed us inside.

Tate's tears subsided, and she calmed enough to release my hand and sit on the couch.

My eyes brimmed with grateful tears. "Lighting the fire was a brilliant idea."

"I canna take the credit for that. By the time I arrived, your oldest had all the lights on and the pit burning."

As I looked at Jessie, I started, newly aware that she was almost my height. She ducked her head. "I saw the marshmallows on the table and remembered. I thought it could guide you home. Mr. McNeil was taking so long. I know you don't like me to light even a candle without supervision, but I had to do something."

Though she rolled her eyes at my protectiveness, I knew she wasn't as sanguine as she wanted to appear.

I tugged her close for a side hug. "It's okay, honey. I forget how mature you are."

"How did you find Tate, Mom?"

"I didn't. A man found her—maybe one of our neighbors." Though he was annoyingly abrupt, I didn't really think the stranger took Tate. Why would he bring her back to me if he had?

Jessie took Tate's hand and whispered in her ear as she draped a quilt from the back of the sofa around her.

Mr. McNeil touched my shoulder in concern. "You sure you're okay, ma'am? Was a long time to be out in the woods."

As he followed me to the foyer, I assured him I was fine. "Do you have any idea who the stranger was?" I described the man in the kilt.

"Aye. Best you avoid that one."

I asked why but he just shook his head.

The door stuck a bit as I pulled it open. "Stay inside, girls. I'm just going to walk Mr. McNeil out," I said, motioning for them to remain there.

We stepped out onto the porch. Embarrassed and now feeling a bit like Chicken Little, I turned to him. "I'm not a survivalist, but I can manage being outdoors for twenty minutes," I said then chuckled.

Mr. McNeil ran a hand through his hair, tousling the locks, and tried to smother a yawn. I regretted inconveniencing him because, after all, we were strangers, and now I repaid his kindness by practically shoving him out the door. So relieved that Tate and I came back safe and sound, I'd had forgotten my manners. "Would you like to come back inside for a glass of water or a beer?"

One side of his mouth quirked up. His eyes shone with something I might have identified as attraction, but I was too tired to be sure and was definitely not up to addressing it tonight if it was.

Before he could respond, I said, "Then again, it looks like Jess woke you up—and I'm sure you must be missing your bed and needing to rise soon."

His grin grew broader and his eyes met mine then traveled southward.

"To wake up early...to get the shop ready..." I fumbled for words, trying to balance my feelings of gratitude with this sudden unease I now felt.

"A bit too early for alcohol, but maybe tea would be nice, non-caffeinated."

His gaze focused on my bare legs. Shocked silent by the obvious interest and maybe misunderstood invitation, I tugged at my jacket, wishing it was longer. At least it covered enough so that my threadbare nightie didn't reveal what hadn't been seen by any male since my husband's death.

The sky transformed from black to a dark, steel blue. *Was I in the woods longer than I thought?* "Wow—actually, maybe another time would be better," I said, striving for graciousness. As I accompanied him to the path which led to town, I remembered what Jessie had told me about a little boy and the barely visible figure I saw. "We need to call the police. Jessie saw a little boy lead Tate into the forest."

Mr. McNeil shook his head. "Your daughter told me, but I'm sure her eyes were playing tricks on her. No one on the island would allow a child out at this time." He stopped so abruptly that I almost ran into him. "Did you see anyone?"

"I thought I did, but now I'm not sure," I answered.

"Lack of sleep can do that. Good night. You get some rest. You dinna want to send the constable on a wild goose chase." He waved as he straddled his motorcycle then revved the engine and motored away.

Inside, I found Jessie sitting beside Tate on the bed in their bedroom. Tate's eyes were at half-mast.

Jessie patted her cheek to wake her and shivered. "Brrr! Mom, she's so cold."

So happy to find her, I didn't think to worry that something may be wrong with Tate. "She might be in shock." I held the back of my hand to her forehead. She didn't feel clammy. "Are you okay, sweetie?"

Despite the warm summer weather, when I took her hand in mine, it was icy.

Tate yawned. "I'm fine, Mommy. Just very tired."

I surreptitiously checked her pulse. It was strong and, if anything, slow. She didn't appear to have any of the signs of shock, except cold skin. She was pale, but only a tad more than usual. I tilted her chin and examined her face. Her pupils weren't dilated, and her breathing seemed normal.

"This night calls for some cocoa. What do you think?"

A ghost of a smile tipped the corners of Jessie's lips as she nodded, but Tate didn't answer.

After patting Tate's back, I told the girls I'd return and went to the kitchen. A few minutes of searching divulged a saucepan. Then I gathered the ingredients I had purchased and made hot chocolate. I coaxed Tate into drinking half a mug. Jessie, of course, finished hers and wanted seconds. I tried to question Tate as she sipped, but she merely yawned at my queries. When it was apparent that she would drink no more, I led her to bed and tucked her in.

"Now, no more visiting the forest alone, Tate Elizabeth," I said, my voice stern.

She nodded and sighed then curled up in a ball with one hand tucked beneath the pillow and the other fisted against her chin. After a visit to the bathroom, Jessie also turned in. She allowed me to tuck her in, which gave away how upset she was.

"Jessie, when you woke up and looked out the window—are you sure you saw a boy?"

"I thought I did, Mom, but it was pretty dark. I asked Tate about it when you walked Mr. McNeil out. She doesn't remember a little boy at all. I didn't make it up, Mom. I really did think I saw him—but I guess I didn't."

"I don't think you were lying, sweetie. I thought I saw something too. I guess we were both just over-tired." I kissed her forehead, eliciting a groan, and said good night.

Once I crawled into bed, I reflected on the event. Jessie and I must have imagined the other figure leading Tate away from the cottage. Maybe she sleep-walked off on her own. I thought again of the man in the woods. Funny how, despite his gruffness and unwelcoming way, when he placed Tate in my arms, I realized he didn't scare me. Though terrified on Tate's account, I knew he wasn't the trigger. Despite the feminist and experienced hiker in me chafing at the way he dismissed me, I felt surprisingly at ease with him.

***

Settled into bed, the girls' window tightly shut, I thought back on our first day here. The people we had met on the island so far were curious, yet kind. When we rode here on the ferry, I hadn't had the correct change. The ferry operator told me not to fret. I could pay what I owed when next I needed to go to the mainland. The only way on or off the island was by boat. Mindful of the prickly plants that lined the path, we walked to the sole village there called, appropriately enough, Thistle. Our first stop upon arriving had been the grocer. The note on the window read "Be Back Soon" in a rushed scrawl. The shop door had been unlocked. We hesitantly entered and gathered our supplies. Before we finished, Mr. McNeil, the owner, returned out of breath. He apologized several times with an adorable grin. I thought him very handsome with his just-shaved look, even the small nick at the dimple in his cheek charmed me. When he turned his head, his hair swept the top of his ears. I guess sleep flattened the curls since it appeared longer when he came to help find Tate. I admired his square jaw line, heavy-brows, and wide forehead. *Strong features,* I had mused. He explained his aunt called, complaining of palpitations, but couldn't find her heart pills, so he ran up the road to find them for her.

Smiling, I remembered his comment. "I'm thinking they're naught but sugar pills. She's healthy as a horse, but to hear it from her, she has one foot in the grave and one foot on a banana peel. She's Doc's best customer, and God forbid he send her home without a concoction of some sort." His Scottish burr, melodic to my ears, had tap danced the chords on my long-forgotten libido. He had bustled about to find what we couldn't and tallied up our bill in record time. Recognizing our American accent, he had helped sack our items, though I assured him I was quite capable.

"Your trolley was chockablock with groceries for a weekend visit," he noted. I explained that we were staying at the cottage for the summer. He smiled and nodded. "Aye, you must be the Shaw family. Mrs. Grant sent word of it."

He gave me his phone number and insisted I call if I needed anything. We didn't have a car and had planned to walk, but the charming Mr. McNeil insisted that his nephew—a pimply, sullen lad with a scraggly beard—give us a ride. My acceptance was one of great appreciation. I had been tired and more than ready to arrive at the rented cottage. The landlady had informed us there were bicycles in the shed for our use, and a small bus made rounds a few times a day to pick up passengers around the island. I think she said it made about a half dozen stops, including a few places in the village, a couple around the countryside, and one at the pier. I looked forward to exploring the quaint village.

When we arrived, the cottage was cleaned and neat. All items we could possibly need were readily available. While inspecting the contents of the medicine cabinet, I had dropped a travel-size tube of toothpaste. When I crouched to pick it up, I found an old-fashioned straight razor that had dropped between the toilet and the sink. The blade was badly rusted, but the ivory handle was carved with beautiful patterns. I could just make out the initial "G" on it. I wondered how such a thing found its way into the hiding place and to whom it belonged. *Why would an elderly lady have such a thing?* She hadn't lived there in a while and, when she did, she lived alone for a long, long time. I knew a local friend of hers still cleaned and stock the place with a few necessities, like toilet paper, bread, and milk.

Thoughts danced through my head and I gave up trying to sleep. My e-reader in hand, feeling like a decadent Roman, I sprawled on the thread-bare chaise in the bedroom's alcove and sipped the dredges of my cocoa. Though the romance was written by one of my favorite authors, I remained distracted. *Who was the raven-haired man in the kilt?*

BAGPIPES AND BASIL
Shrouded Isle, Scotland

I had just put the appetizers on the table when the unmistakable, high-pitched scream of a teenage girl pierced my skull like an icepick. "Please, let no one be hurt," I prayed as I raced outside. Our new pet kitten, Tabby, followed, narrowly avoiding the closing door. Not wanting to risk losing her again, I swept her up before she scampered away. She was still so small that I could tuck her in my apron pocket. She snuggled in one corner with only her head peeking over the top. I held her close to my stomach and ran, following the sounds of raised children's voices.

"Get it off me!" I heard Grace cried out as I rounded the corner. The guests stood by the open shed door. An enormous, crow-like bird cawed and dive-bombed Grace. She waved her arms overhead as she ducked and weaved around the yard. Gavin brandished a hoe, but he couldn't strike the bird without risking hitting Grace.

It had to be Grace. She'd been a thorn in my daughters' rose bouquet of a party from the moment she arrived.

"That's what you get for teasing it!" my youngest, Tate, said. She leaned against the shed wall, her arms tightly folded against her body as the other agitated guests shouted and corralled the bird and girl. The kitten leapt from my apron pocket, landing so close to Grace that I feared she'd get trod upon. Tabby firmly planted her four tiny paws and hissed. The bird fluttered to the ground. Light hit its iridescent feathers as it strutted toward the kitten.

Tate's older sister, Jessie, dashed between the kitten and the bird. Little Tabby almost vanished in Jess's shadow. "Don't you dare hurt my cat."

Grace's sweaty face beamed beet red. "You're trying to keep that stupid cat safe? You didn't help me!"

Jessie bristled and tossed a glare back at her guest. "At least the cat has enough sense to stay still. We couldn't help you because you wouldn't stop running."

Jessie watched the bird as she backed away. "Nice birdie. You don't want to eat a cat," she crooned. Keeping her eye on the creature, she eased the kitten into her arms.

Greg, my—dare I say it—boyfriend, joined us. *Boyfriend.* Even saying it in my head made me feel a combination of embarrassment and giddiness. Once Grace and the rest of the children had calmed, the bird ceased its fluttering and cocked its head first one way, then the other as it regarded us.

"Steady now. No one move. The oozlum bird is a sma fae, but a silly creature that wouldna hurt a fly." We'd known each other for only a few months, yet the sound of Greg's Scottish burr still set my heart aflutter. Greg inhaled, but before he could speak, I gripped his arm.

"Let me try to send it back," I whispered.

The crease between his eyes deepened. "I dinna think ye ready yet."

"But I'm supposed to share the duties of Keeper of the Forest. Shouldn't I be able to banish fae back to the Hill?" If we ever fail to follow through with our duties, the fae could attack mankind, putting the world in peril.

From Jessie's arms, the kitten eyed the bird and meowed at it. The bird answered her with a throaty croak.

I thought our conversation had been stealthy, but the children were no longer talking amongst themselves and watching the bird. Now they were looking at me.

Greg shrugged, the worn cotton of his shirt stretching across his broad shoulders. "Good a time as any. The bird is harmless."

I cast my mind back to all the times I had witnessed Greg banishing fae. He was always so self-assured. But then, he had been doing it for hundreds of years. I cleared my throat, deepen my voice, and said, "Begone, little fae!"

The bird ruffled its feathers and preened.

Okay, guess I'll try again. I clapped to get its attention, then bellowed, "Go back to your world!"

The bird took wing but instead of fleeing, it circled my head, then landed on my shoulder. I staggered at the weight.

"*Chirp?*" it said in my ear, the volume loud enough to startle me. At the movement, the bird's grip tightened. I winced as the talons jabbed my shoulder. This close, I more readily understood Grace's reaction. The tip of the humongous, curved black beak brushed against my hair as the oozlum turned its head. I imagined it snapping off my nose and shuddered. Out of the corner of my eyes, I could see the children exchanging barely suppressed smiles. I suppose I did look silly.

"Off with ye!" Greg said to the bird and flapped his hands at the oozlum like a circus performer. Since he'd never done so before, I guess he was trying to divert attention from my lame attempt. The bird flapped its wings, clipping my head.

Then it winged upwards, making tighter and tighter circles. The oozlum wheeled faster until the creature blurred and its beak seemed to meet its tail. With a swirl of feathers, it cawed raucously, then disappeared. Just before it vanished, a large, white glob dropped.

Splat! Grace caterwauled as bird poop landed on her shoulder with enough force to splatter her cheek. "Eww!" She waved her hand at her arm as if she could scare the stain away.

I whisked off my apron and handed it to her.

Tate giggled. "At least it didn't land on your head."

Since Grace was only smearing the stain further down the front of her blouse, I stopped her and reclaimed the apron. "You can borrow a shirt from Jessie, and while you're eating, I'll wash yours."

Grace shuddered. "I'm going inside before something else attacks me."

"It was just a silly bird attracted to silly people," Tate muttered.

Uh oh. I ignored the remark. I thought I was the only person who heard it. Over the summer and fall my youngest, Tate, had gained three inches and fifteen pounds. The extra weight curved her hips. Along with needing larger clothing, future bra shopping loomed. Tate no longer had the flat chest of a child and, if one looked closely, and I hoped no one was, her nipples were perky in the cooler air.

Okay, Becca, it's past time.

Jessie, my oldest, had been a late bloomer. When puberty hit, she remained slender but went through a gawky, newborn colt stage. I could see Tate would have a more turbulent experience with her teen years, and I hoped to help her get through the transitory phase.

I asked Grace if the bird had hurt her, but the girl insisted she was fine. It looked like she had only sustained a disheveled head of hair and a poopy shirt. Grace was embarrassed and sullen, a terrible combination. I got her to sit on the yard chair farthest from the shed and lent her the ponytail holder from around my wrist so she could put up her hair to keep it out of the poop.

"When did the bird appear?" Greg asked.

Tate pushed away from the wall. "A clue was in the shed. Everyone solved it at the same time—or some could have just chased after the groups that knew where to go." Her eyes narrowed as she pointedly looked at Grace.

"'Tis one of the lesser fae creatures and has little magic," Greg said.

Gavin stepped forward. "I've seen it in our fields. We put out extra corn so it won't steal from the chickens. Aside from that and being a bit distracting with its loud noises and silly antics, it hurts nobody or anything." Several of the other children nodded in agreement.

Grace stood with her arms akimbo. "*I've* never seen it before."

"Me neither," Lundy said, rubbing his arms, Scotland's fall weather bringing goosebumps to his uncovered skin. He wasn't the most vocal teen in the world, so it surprised me that he commented.

Gavin shrugged. "Probably because you both live in the village. It mostly shows up in the countryside."

"Aye. I havena needed to chase it back. Once seen, it's always returned on its own," Greg said.

I wish he had shared that tidbit with me earlier.

"Then why did it stick around and attack me?" Grace asked.

"Because you poked at it with a rake instead of just waiting for it to fly out of the shed," Tate retorted. Elspeth, Grace's little sister, tugged at Tate's arm, but Tate shrugged her off.

Eager to defuse the situation, I said, "No harm done. Have you found all the clues?"

"This is the last one—the one that leads to the treasure," Jessie answered. "So, who knows the answer?"

Several voices chimed in.

"It looks like there'll be multiple winners," I said. Jessie and I had discussed this possibility and decided the "everyone's a winner" approach would be better than rewarding only one group.

The last clue was in code, but earlier clues hinted the key to breaking it. Within a few moments of scribbling on their notepads, they were all able to answer.

Grace rolled her eyes. "*Back to the house, cheese for a mouse.* I bet the prize is just gonna be cheesy macaroni for dinner."

"Wrong, Grace. Pizza's for dinner and that isn't the prize. Everyone will find out what it is after we eat." Tate tossed out the comment as she walked past the girl.

"Pizza!" the children exclaimed.

I barely avoided being trampled as the group rushed toward the back door.

Greg slipped his arm around me. "Pizza?" he asked.

I hadn't been aware of how cold I was without a jacket until his proximity warmed me. "Never had it?"

"Nae."

"Then you're in for a treat." As we followed them, I noticed seed scattered on the ground in front of the shed.

***

Earlier that day

The day had started off well enough. Jessie and Tate spent the morning hiding the clues and decorating while I meal prepped as much as I could before the guests arrived. As the number of children rapidly increased, I doubted the wisdom of letting the girls send out so many invitations, especially after Elspeth and Grace arrived. I don't know what got into the two of them. Elspeth couldn't sit still and kept looking to her sister for... approval? I wasn't sure. And Grace, Grace needled Jess every chance she got.

Ugh. Twelve kids. I shook my head. Why did I agree to it? No, it was worse: I had *suggested* it.

That summer, my oldest daughter, Jessica, ruined what should have been a fun teen get-together. Instead of a night on the mainland to see a movie, Jessie humiliated Lundy, the grocer's nephew, who had such a crush on Jessie that he drove her nuts. Thanks to her efforts, she'd lost her appeal to him. However, her actions upset the other guests. *Apparently my lack of social skills did not pass a generation.*

I convinced Jessie to postpone the party until after school started. The group that passed for the Shrouded Island School District school board hired me as new head teacher, and I hoped to get to know the students before they gathered at our home. My duties mirrored the volunteering I did as a parent for the kids' schools when they were young. Thankfully, the previous head teacher had done the vast majority of the first-of-the-school-year work during the summer. She'd agreed to help for a few months while I accustomed myself to the position. I'd taught school but had never held an administrative position. So far, I'd done a lot of busy work that didn't utilize my experience as a teacher and history degree graduate.

I still couldn't get accustomed to the fact that we stayed. What should have been a summer getaway to the tiny Scottish island turned into a new home and job. My two daughters and I had first moved to Scotland to be somewhere where we could grieve the loss of David, my husband, their dad. I took a job as a teacher at the American school in Aberdeen, Scotland. I only planned to be there a year, but the lifestyle suited us to a tee. By the time summer break arrived, I had already planned to stay in the country at least until Jessie, my oldest daughter, graduated from high school to take advantage of the International Baccalaureate, a program that prepared students to be accepted at universities worldwide. Then I treated the girls to a vacation.

During this vacation, I had learned fairies exist, and they weren't all friendly, like Tinkerbell. Looking back on it, Tinkerbell wasn't always a glittery ball of sunshine either. The fairies, or fae, as they prefer to be called, lived in a hill in a forest on the Shrouded Isle, the place destined to be our new home. One islander, Greg Gillie, was charged with making sure the fae remained in the Hill. He excelled at the job for hundreds of years—and then we arrived.

After the deaths of Greg's wife and child in the late eighteenth century, grief consumed him to the point that he no longer cared for others, so he was cursed to remain in the forest and keep the peace between the fae and the islanders. The curse would be in effect until the Ghillie, as he came to be known, learned to change his selfish ways and care for another.

As Greg and I became attracted to each other, the magical promise called the geas that gave Greg the duty and ability to protect all from the fae weakened. Magical creatures escaped and menaced the island until we expressed our feelings for one another, and I agreed to remain on the island to help Greg with his duties. When I put it like that, it sounds as though it should be a piece of cake. Trust me, it isn't. I still don't know what role I play in "helping" Greg with his task.

Once all our guests arrived, I gave them time to socialize. I did a quick count of heads every now and then which meant, worrywart that I am, I was tallying every ten minutes. Despite my niggling doubts, I had faith that the party would be a success. I'm such an optimist. *Sigh.*

The two doctors' daughters, Nessa, who was Jessie's age, and Jody, who was the same age as my youngest daughter, Tate, sat on the bench outside the door. In a corner, Gavin and Jessie chatted. There had been no cooling off of the budding romance, even though Gavin quit school to work full time with his dad. Gavin seemed to be a nice young man, but I worried Jessie hadn't any close girlfriends. As the school year progressed, even Tate was having issues with her classmates. She spent a lot of time at Elspeth's home, but when she spoke about her, Tate didn't seem to like her all that much.

Lundy and two of the other boys milled about outside, bouncing a ball back and forth between them. I hoped Lundy wasn't carrying a grudge. He had a crush on Jessie from day one, much like his uncle had had on me. Lundy looked grumpy, but then again, he looked that way most of the time.

Pastor Doyles' sons were only a year apart in age. They resembled each other so much that I still had a hard time telling them apart and suspected they purposely misled me. Both had wavy brown hair and chubby cheeks. One had a mole just above his upper lip, but I constantly forgot which.

Like most pastor kids I'd ever been around, when mischief occurred, the Doyles boys were near more often than not. One of the boy's names was Bean, short for Beathan. His brother, Anthony, was called Ant. Marnie's two daughters, Elspeth and Grace, were easily identifiable thanks to the bright red hair. They hung around Tate.

Uh oh. I couldn't see Rabbie or Nora. Those two had been boyfriend and girlfriend forever, according to the girls. I had already caught them making out once.

I heaved open the window and leaned out, searching for the couple. I espied them, arms wrapped around each other, behind the garden shed. "Ahem! If you two can't keep your hands off one another, I'm having Tate chaperone," I warned them. Both blushed as red as the Wallace girls' hair and joined the other guests.

When Greg offered to help with the party, I accepted. Jess, while being respectful, made it clearly known that she would prefer he didn't, so he tried to limit his aid to behind-the-scenes duties. So far, she was reluctantly accepting the budding relationship between Greg and I, but I predicted a blow up at some point. It probably would have occurred earlier if it weren't for her needing to be on her best behavior to have the party.

When I told the girls we were staying, I explained how there would be no one guarding the fae borders if Greg and I had not agreed to act as Keepers. I kinda fudged the part where I could have left and Greg would have continued to carry out his duties as he had for years alone. We could never speak again. I couldn't relinquish our budding relationship, so I stayed. Tate nodded and went on about her business. Jessie, though polite, wasn't very enthused.

Surely Jess was ready to start the scavenger hunt. Goodness knows I was. "Jess, come here," I called. She rose on her tiptoes and leaned close to Gavin. I was pretty sure she kissed his cheek, but her long, purple-black hair obscured my view.

Once Jessie entered the house and closed the door, she said, "What?" She eyed Gavin through the window and frowned when Grace tried to sneak up on him. Gavin spun around just in time to prevent what looked like a tickle attack. He good-naturedly laughed as the girl giggled and Jessie blew out a breath.

I cleared my throat. "Jessie? Can I have your entire attention?"

Giving me stink eye, she said, "I'm standing right here, Mom. Just tell me what you want." At least the tone of voice was pleasant enough.

"Are you ready to start the hunt?"

Much as I had a moment earlier, Jessie did a quick head count. "Yes, I think so." She called out the door, "Hey y'all, come here!"

The older guests slowly shuffled in our direction. The younger ones galloped over and skittered around like frisky ponies.

Though the Shrouded Isle was small, I hoped the guests walking the parameters as they searched for clues would consume a considerable amount of time. Conall McNeil, the grocer, had agreed to help watch them when they were in town. He reluctantly accepted that his romantic inclinations toward me would not go into fruition—I thought.

When I had the attentions of all the guests, I cleared my throat and read off the paper my daughter had prepared for me.

After I gave the first clue to the hunt, the guests, divided into teams, immediately ran off. I noted that the smallest group was my daughter and her boyfriend. There were three other groups, two groups of three and one with four. Since Jess helped plan the treasure hunt, she couldn't help Gavin, so he was on his own. I guess he was also on the village kids' blacklist.

As I watched Tate race down the lane, I wondered at how much better she was doing these days. She'd had health issues all her life. We held her back, so she started kindergarten a year later than she should have. It worked out since she was always so much smaller than the kids her age, not that you could tell it now. It had seemed like she was outgrowing her problems. We hadn't been to an emergency room in months.

Tate's cheeks pinked with excitement as she skipped, holding hands with Jody and Elspeth. To my surprise, Grace had joined the group of younger kids.

Tate blossomed before my eyes. That happened to my best friend. School ended, and she looked like a kid. At the beginning of the following year, she was wearing a B-cup, gained two inches and hips. It was very noticeable to the kids who hadn't seen her all summer. In fact, students accused my friend of stuffing her bra, but I had time to adjust to it and didn't really realize how great the difference was until that moment when she got off the school bus in her new clothes.

The children drifted off like wind-swept, cottony dandelion seeds when I noticed a kilt-clad form standing beneath the old oak tree on the border of the cottage yard. Greg stepped out from the shade and smiled at me. A feeling bloomed in my heart, one that I refused to call love—it was too soon for that. As he approached, I realized I was no longer worried about the status of the children's party. I ducked my head to conceal my goofy grin and remembered I had stationed him there for a reason. I asked, "Have they all figured out the clue?"

"Aye, they've taken to the garden where they will find the next one. How has it gone?"

"Well—I don't know."

He closed the distance between us and gathered me into his arms. "What has you fretting?"

I shivered and willed myself not to snuggle closer. Though my body still wasn't accustomed to the cool autumns, I loved watching the green leaves seem to turn to glowing shades of red, orange, and yellow overnight.

"Jessie doesn't seem to have any friends. The only person in her group is Gavin. Even Nessa seems to have abandoned her. And I think Gavin is being shunned, too."

"Shunned? 'Tis an old term. You think it fitting?"

I fell back and watched him cock his head as one corner of his mouth twitched, revealing the amusement he felt. "Aye," I mocked him with an exaggerated accent.

"Yon Jessica will land on her feet like a cat," he said as Jessica and Gavin sprinted past toward the road passing Kay.

Kay was our nearest neighbor and the first friend I made on the island. She brushed her hands down her skirt, one she no doubt made herself. She'd sewn pieces of tartan, different but each containing the color red, into a patchwork midi. Instead of looking busy and ridiculous, it looked festively bohemian. Kay used her creative skills to make products sold in a local shop. Today, her hair was in a French braid. Had someone done it for her? I could never fix my unruly brown curls like that. I'd tried braiding Tate's hair since hers is the same length and wavy like mine, thinking it might be easier to learn how on someone else's tresses. No luck.

Greg and I waited at the door of the cottage. When Kay reached us, I said, "I thought you were working at the tea shop today."

"No, not today. Things are quieting down now that the tourist season is over and Marnie doesn't need me as often." She turned to Greg. "And you, how do you fare?"

"Nae bad."

Kay crossed her arms, her gaze focused somewhere in the distance, and she fidgeted for a moment before taking a deep breath. "I know you have a new arrangement with Herne, but I still feel unrest in the forest."

"Aye? We hadna fae out and aboot except the wee ones. What is this unrest you speak of?" Greg asked.

Kay's gesture included both of us. "You are human. I am part fae. Please don't discount what I say if you aren't feeling it, too. I know each of you has a power. You have your witchcraft, Becca—" She nodded at me, then turned to Greg. "—and you, Greg, have the powers invested to you by Herne, but you aren't fae and don't have as close of a relationship to the land that people with fae blood do."

It bothered me that Kay said only Greg had the powers of the Keeper of the Forest. I thought we were both Keepers. Did I misunderstand?

While on the island, I had discovered that one of my ancestors had come from here. Like most of the people on the island, Kay came here because she was different. In this case, she was a witch. This skill had been passed down to me and my daughters. We were the first of our family in generations to develop it, that I know of, anyway.

"Have you spoken to the others?" Greg asked. By others, I supposed he meant the islanders who also shared her ties to the fae.

"Yes, and they feel it, too."

Greg nodded. "I will keep watch, but I've nae seen anything amiss. If you sense anything more specific, anything I can act against, let me know."

Many of the islanders had fae blood and special powers, but I was still a stranger and they were slow to confide. On my way out, I picked the keys from the hook that hung by the door. "I hate to rush you off, but I don't want to let the kids get too far ahead of me. There's a list of all their stops. I'm going to catch the bus to the village. The girls hid most of the clues there." Though I felt funny about it since most of the village seemed to eschew locked doors, I let Kay and Greg precede me out and stuck the old-fashioned key in the keyhole, then gave it a sharp twist.

Turning toward me and winking so Kay couldn't see, Greg said, "I dinna think you need do this, Rebecca. You and your girls are safe here. The village is small. Everyone knows everyone else."

"I know. But I'd rather keep my eye on them—at least part of the time." *Everyone who's lived here forever knows everyone else. We're new and don't fit in yet.*

Kay paused on the porch. "I'll be seeing you, then. I've been feeling uneasy about it and felt I was overdue mentioning my worries. Mind what I say, you two. Perhaps the danger is from without instead of within, and Becca's skills will be needed to address it."

I pocketed the keys and snorted. "If my witchcraft is supposed to help, we're in trouble."

"You come by the skill naturally. You just need a wee bit of coaching. I've got you started, but Amberlee is the expert. She's an excellent teacher. With time, you'll be casting spells with the best of them." Kay chuckled and winked.

Amberlee, a friend from Kay's past who she had recently found again, was a very strong witch. Since they had reconnected, she moved in with Kay. I wondered about the dynamics of their relationship but didn't feel I knew either of them enough to ask. "I'm so glad she's agreed to help us, but I wish she'd let me pay her for her time. She may feel I am taking advantage of her."

"No worries there. She's enjoying it." Kay tsked and shook her head. "Although it does take up a lot of her time," she added in a low enough voice that I wondered if she meant for me to hear. She shook her head and smiled at me. "Goodness, manners are one thing, but you fret too much." Her forehead crinkled for a moment, and her mouth formed a small frown that she quickly reversed. "However, Amberlee is looking for a job, and once she finds one, she'll need to cut back on how much time she spends teaching you and Jess. As it is, I feel like I hardly get to see her, even though she's living with me." She brushed her palms together. "Oh well, I'm experimenting with bread flavoring today. If it's a success, I'll bring you some tomorrow and you can give me your opinion."

Unlike me, Kay often baked, and not only at the tea shop, but at home, too. "Can't wait. I'll see you later then. Bye."

Greg sketched a wave and Kay continued to her cottage located down the lane from ours.

I turned to Greg, who remained on the porch. "Aren't you coming? I don't plan on being gone long."

"Nae, I will stay. I am guessing we'll have twelve hungry, thirsty young people afterwards."

"Guess I don't need to lock the door. I can always ring you if I end up staying away longer than I thought I would." I reopened it and we went inside.

Greg pointed to the phone. "You mean you'll call me?" Frowning, he looked at the black, old-fashioned rotary device and gingerly placed a hand on it. "All I need to do is pick it up and hold it?"

"Pick it up now. It won't bite."

"But it's nae ringing—"

"At some point, you'll want to make a phone call, Greg."

"I havena needed to in over two hundred years. I see naught a reason I would need to now."

Greg was one of the original settlers on the island. When the fae king tasked him with protecting the islanders from the fae, he ceased aging and his longevity increased.

I shook my head. Greg was turning out to be quite the technophobe. All the devices and the things that they did amazed him, but so far, I hadn't been able to talk him into even using my Kindle to read. And he was quite the reader. He was better about the kitchen. The stove was gas, and he seemed okay with it, and the toilet, thank goodness. He had lived in the forest for hundreds of years with no modern conveniences, held there by the power of the king of fairies.

I walked to the bus stop. I knew the kids would arrive at the village via a wagon towed by the Samms' tractor and, since its top speed is about twenty miles per hour, they'd be creeping along the road.

***

The bus had only three passengers when I got on, but by the time we drove into the village, few empty seats would remain. Tourism waned with the beginning of the school year and the cool weather, but since it was a Saturday, the islanders and visitors were out and about.

The bus passed the tractor, which had just pulled out onto the street. The bus driver, wearing his customary loosened blue tie and the matching cap that he always tugged low on his forehead, honked the horn, and the children whooped and waved. Normally somewhat dour, he surprised me.

After we arrived at the village, I sat on the bus stop bench and waited. I had a good view and could easily see the tractor approach. Mr. Samms didn't intend to drive through the village. He would drop the kids off on the outskirts. When I saw them making their way down the road, I rushed to a portion of stone wall partially obscured by trees and bushes and sat on a rough corner. They shouldn't notice me at all unless they were looking for me—and they wouldn't be. Unfortunately, I wouldn't be able to see them very well either.

I heard the murmurs of conversation, then one voice rang out. "I don't think it's fair that you're Gavin's partner. You probably give him hints where to look." I recognized the speaker. Unsurprisingly, it was Grace.

"She does not. It's just because I know her better that I can guess more easily. You're just mad because you can't figure any of it out and are just following everybody else."

I smiled at Gavin's defense.

"She shouldn't be taking part at all. She made it up so she knows where everything is," Grace complained. There were a few assents. I thought I heard Lundy's voice muttering, "Aye."

"It's *her* party. Did you expect her to stay home while the rest of us had fun?" Gavin retorted.

"Jessie worked real hard on this because she wanted you all to have a great time and she would *never* cheat," Tate pointed out. "You're just being mean."

Jessie cleared her throat and said, "You can be in our group, Grace." *Good girl, Jessie!*

"How many clues are there?" Grace asked.

"There's a dozen, and we've only found four," Jessie answered.

"Okay, I guess I could do that," Grace said. "If it's okay." I think she was striving for nonchalance, but I could hear excitement in her voice.

Jody complained that with Grace gone, Tate's group would be the only one comprising of all younger kids. Though Elspeth sided with Jody, Tate remained silent. I'd thought it odd that Grace had been spending most of her time with Tate and joined her and her friends to make a group. I wondered if she had done so, planning to weasel her way into Gavin and Jessie's group later. If so, Tate and her friends would be better off without a brooding teammate who didn't want to be there.

They must have come to the same conclusion, because the arguing soon stopped and Grace called out, "Okay, then. Come on, Gavin, we have clues to find!"

The voices faded as the kids moved farther and farther away. I waited until I was sure all of them had passed my hiding place, then risked a look. At the very back of the group, Jessie walked, her arms folded across her chest. Nora and Rabbie were in the back, too, but completely wrapped up in each other and stealing kisses when they thought no one was looking. Though Nessa was in their group, she lit up as she chatted to Lundy who barely paid her mind, giving evidence that she still was crushing on him and he was still uninterested in her, while the Doyles brothers, who were in Lundy's group, were in engaged in some game. It looked like the sole goal was to knock the other down.

Tate, Jody and Elspeth rushed ahead, whispering to each other, hoping to get a jump on the other groups. Tate snuck a glance back at Jess, then wrinkled her nose at Nobbie's—or should it be Rora's?—PDA.

Oh, Jessie. My heart went out for my oldest. I hoped the party wasn't a mistake. If she had agreed to just have a movie party, the kids' attentions would be focused on the screen and it would be less unlikely for pairing-offs to occur.

I stood on my tiptoes, searching for Gavin's blond head. Resigned that I was too short, I climbed on the wall and caught sight of him near the front. Grace had a death grip on his arm. Gavin turned back now and then, his eyes searching out Jessie, face troubled.

"Parties like this were a lot easier when the kids were still in grammar school," I grumbled. I hopped off the wall and continued to follow the kids, trying to stay far enough back so as not to be noticed.

The next clue led them into the grocer. I didn't enter. I planned to follow and make sure they all made it back to where Gavin's dad, Mr. Samms, parked the tractor. He would drive them back to the cottage. Tate had wanted to have some clues lead into the forest, but I ixnayed that right away. The last thing I needed was to have to call a parent and explain I lost a child in the woods. Even if the tractor beat me back, Greg was there and he would monitor the group.

It seemed as though the kids had been inside for only a moment before Grace flew out of the shop tugging a puzzled Gavin behind her. "Wait! We left without Jessie," he said.

"Oh, she'll catch up. After all, she knows all the answers to the clues. Anyway, don't you want to win? The Americans can't help but be over the top. Look at all the hoopla involved in a simple party. You would think Jessie was Meghan Markle. I'm sure the prize will be something brill." She glanced in the plate glass window of the grocer, catching her reflection in it, and surreptitiously tugged her blouse lower, then grabbed Gavin's hand again and tugged him down the small alley leading to the back door. I followed and ducked behind a trash dumpster.

Gavin allowed himself to be led but was clearly suspicious. "Are you sure you know the answer?"

"It's a dead easy puzzle. I know exactly where the next clue is. It's not far. Anyway, if I'm wrong, somehow, we have to end up at the cottage, so we'll just go back." Grace and Gavin disappeared around the corner just as the other kids exited. As a whole, they passed the alleyway and ran down the block toward the doctor's office. Once they were out of sight, hearing voices, I peeked down the alley. I really didn't want to be caught spying but was too curious to find out what Grace was up to. Conall kept his shop and the area around it tidy. Nothing for me to trip over. It also meant that if the kids doubled back, they would catch me. I'd risk it. I was an adult and didn't need to apologize for checking up on my guests. *No blushing, Becca!*

"Come on, Gavin. We really don't need to get back right away. Let's hang out here and talk. Jessie knows all the answers. We don't need to find all the clues. No one else will ever know if we don't. They'll think we're far ahead or behind or whatever."

"That wouldn't be fair to Jess. She really wanted to do something special for everyone and worked hard on this. She felt awful about Lundy and messing up the evening for everyone."

"You know the reason she's doing all this, don't you? She only cares about you. She wants to look good in your eyes. She doesn't care about any of the rest of us."

"Yes, she does. Come on." Gavin paused, then let out an exasperated sigh. "Everyone's ahead of us now. We're going to need to step it up and get cracking if we want to win, because I'm not going to Jessie for the answers."

I gave a fist pump. *Go Gavin!*

Grace blocked Gavin's view, forcing him to look at her. "You know, Jess won't be here forever. She'll leave as soon as she graduates. You aren't going anywhere, Gavin. You'll stay here—with us, with me."

"She might stay. Or she might go off to college and return here. You don't know that."

"If you believe that, you're fooling yourself. She'll leave and she won't come back except to visit her mom. If her mom stays."

"What do you mean by that?"

Grace lowered her voice. "Gavin, honestly. Why would she want to stay here?"

"Because—because she cares about Mr. Gillie."

"This place is boring. She's lived in Aberdeen. In Houston. Do you really think she wants to stay here?"

"If she really loves him, she will."

"If he really loved her, he'd go."

"You know that isn't possible."

"Why are we talking about this? It has nothing to do with us. If Jessie leaves and never comes back, that's her decision, and good riddance. *I'm* not begging her to stay."

Hearing a scuffling of footsteps, I looked for a place to hide but I didn't need to. Gavin was so deep in thought that he didn't even notice me crouched behind the bin, and Grace was so self-satisfied that she didn't see me either.

I didn't want to be involved in my daughter's love life, but this was...wrong. I didn't know what I should do about, it but I wanted to do something. Like squish Grace.

"Why are you so sure you'll be staying here?" Gavin asked.

"Because my fae blood has revealed itself." I watched as Grace pulled her hand from her pocket, whispered something, and brushed her knuckle on a scrape on Gavin's cheek—probably one he got from shaving. I watched as the dots of dried blood vanished and the redness faded. The wound healed so fast that it was as if I was watching a fast-forwarded scene like the one that shows a blossom unfurl in seconds.

Grace smiled in triumph, her heart-shaped face beaming. "The magic of my family is of the hearth."

Magic? Were the Wallaces part fae, too? I'd have to ask Greg or Kay about it later.

Gavin rubbed his cheek for a moment, then his chin jerked up and he stared at Grace. "That isn't hearth magic. Did you buy a charm?"

Grace ran her hands over the legs of her jeans. Were her palms sweaty?

"I didn't buy anything, Gavin. I really can do magic like the fae." When she leaned in closer to him, I noticed how low cut her blouse was. Not indecently so, I guess, but she had achieved cleavage by squeezing her arms tight to her body. He bowed his head. I hoped he didn't notice the boobage, but if I could from so far away, it was pretty sure he did. "And like the fae, I don't have to be good," she whispered.

I wished I was anywhere but here. Darn my curiosity! *Don't kiss her, don't kiss her—please don't. At least until after you've broken up with Jess.*

Spring Shenanigans
The Shrouded Isle
Zoe Tasia

This is a work of fiction. Similarities to real people, places, or events are entirely coincidental.

SPRING SHENANIGANS
First edition. October 31, 2018.
Copyright © 2018 Zoe Tasia.
ISBN: 978-1393997283
Written by Zoe Tasia.

SPRING SHENANIGANS

"Help, help me!" The voice was the high, unmistakable lilt of a young child. Young enough that Greg couldn't tell if the wee one was a lad or lassie, especially since panic made the timbre higher. He rolled out of the large, hollowed-out trunk that served as his bed. The tree seemed to warm against his back as it propelled him gently from his feathered nest and the threadbare blanket.

Soft ropey strands bounced off his cheeks when he shook his head. "What's this?" For a moment he thought of Medusa and her snakes, but after a moment of panic, he realized the strands were too small and not animated. He reached up and nabbed one, running two fingers down its length. Before he brought it close enough to eyeball, he recognized the feel, though his wife had never plaited her hair into more than two and he felt dozens. "Who braided my hair?" he asked, though no one was there to answer. He heard the child call out once more.

He would have to deal with his coif later. *I must look like a gowk.*

As he strode toward the sound, he felt his eyes dilate and he knew if he had a mirror handy, the irises had vanished except for a small ring of green. His vision blurred for a moment adjusting, then his surroundings showed in sharp relief. He

scanned the forest. Glimmering dots shimmered in the distance. As he drew near, his eyes adjusted once more to the extra light and he could tell the pupils shrunk and appeared more normal. "Hello? Where are you?" He gasped when a small hand grasped his calf.

A lad about the age that his daughter was when he lost her scrambled out of a gorse bush. The coconutty-almond scent wafted from the stirred blossoms. The child was covered with butter-yellow petals and spines from the stems that snagged his homespun clothes. As he struggled, ripe flower pods burst in the warm night sprinkling him with their seeds. Pointing to blue lights in the distance, the lad said, "They've taken my sister, sir. You've got to help me." He tugged his leg to free himself, but only succeeded in tearing the hem of his pants.

"Stay still, now. I will free you." Keeping his eyes on the unnatural flickers and judging they were not dimming, he dropped to one knee. Although the pricks from the plant's thorns must hurt, the brave lad staved off tears. Greg worked quickly with his knife, slicing through the plant. As he did so, he asked, "What is your name?"

The child shuddered like a frightened rabbit until he got a closer look at Greg's head. "I'm Iain." Curiosity trumped his fear. He gingerly poked one of Greg's braids. "Why is your hair in knots?"

Greg took the child's chin and tilted his face so they were eye to eye. "Never you mind that, young Master Iain. What happened? Tell me quickly."

The boy swallowed. "Jilly was playing with her rag doll. I was supposed to be watching her. I saw a dun horse prancing—it wore a gilded saddle and had a white plume betwixt its ears. Its mane was all twisty like your hair." Shaking his head, a look of amazement crossed Iain's face. "It was so wondrous that I couldna take my eyes off it. Jilly wasna but a few feet away from me. One moment, she was fine. Then she was crying and saying they took her dolly—that they flew away with it. 'Twas hard to understand her through the tears." The lad brushed at the petals that clung to him. "She said they were wee creatures and fled to the forest and I thought I would just go and look for a bit. Me mum would be furious to find out I had let my attention stray and Jilly was abawlin' as if Christmas Day had been cancelled. Jilly wouldn't stay near our cottage and I didna want to leave her alone, so we went together. I swear we only took two steps past the woods, but somehow, we got turned around and then it got dark. Those yonder little creatures ventured forth and sung us a song and we went sleepy like, but not asleep. They had spread cloaks on the ground and Jilly dropped on hers, but I rolled into the gorse bush. They tried to budge me, but I was too heavy for them to lift. They carried my sister away. They left and then sleep left me, so I called out, hopin' someone would hear."

Greg didn't know what stripe of animals stole the doll, but no bird that he knew of had wings that shined and lit the night sky. Perhaps these creatures were some of those he was warned about. "You best stay with me but do exactly what I tell you to. I don't know what evils this forest holds." He turned to follow the lights.

New to his duties as Keeper of the Forest, Greg wasn't entirely sure what was expected of him. He had no mentor. As far as he knew, he was the first and possibly, only. After the tragedy, he cared about nothing, so caught up in his grief he had only been able to mourn his beloved wife and child. Though he was still saddened beyond measure, now he couldn't help but wonder what he was supposed to do. He was told only to keep to the forest and protect the villagers from the menaces living there.

Before he and his family moved into their home, they heard tales from the mainlanders about the island—children who went missing and men found dead, but the cause not always evident. In the case of John Douglas, he appeared to have aged fifty years in the course of an evening. Greg had thought it was a case of mistaken identity, but the widow swore that the odd heart-shaped mole on the back of his ear confirmed, at least to her, that the corpse was that of her husband. She said he would never have left her and the bairns when some of the womenfolk gently suggested it. She took with her the body and hied to the mainland, afraid that whatever had gotten to her Johnny would come after her children next.

The Douglas family had cleared an area near the forest. The empty home, one of many, remained.

Greg and his wife and child had been among the first to colonize the island—at least of recent. The mainlanders had warned them off, saying rare was the man who lived to return. Greg and his wife thought that they merely didna want Highlanders living so near, fearing they would bring the wrath of the English down upon their loyalists' heads. Perhaps it was more than that, though.

Over the brief spell of time they were on the island, new homes and businesses rose exponentially. The weather was cooling and no one wanted to be without shelter. It was not much longer than past the time when the seventh home was built that strange things occurred. Cows stopped giving milk. Items went missing, then reappeared in strange places.

Greg, himself was caught up in his own work, settling his family and making sure that none harassed his wife. She was a rare sort. Much loved by him, but odd and sickly. Many bedeviled her, so they found this secluded island to live, away from superstitious mobs. Many of the islanders were of the same bent. They wanted to be left alone in peace, and Greg was happy to do so.

Then tragedy struck and he abandoned his home and the community to live in the forest, avoiding all. Time meant nothing to him. Long, gray hours became long gray days, weeks, and months, until he could barely recall living differently. And then, the creature came to him. It appeared in mannish form but Greg ken it was no man that spoke to him. The creature rode a red-eyed steed and monstrous dogs accompanied it. It struck fear in Greg's heart.

As the creature spoke, he felt only disbelief and confusion. When the being turned to depart, a wave of dizziness unbalanced him. He reeled, then his bones seemed to burn and every muscle in his body tightened. Just before he collapsed, he smelled the sharp scent of ozone. Afterwards he discovered that he had extraordinary new abilities. He could travel across the forest at great speeds, faster than the fastest horse. He could see in the dark. Animals no longer feared him. He felt guilty about killing them so he might eat and said a brief prayer each time that it would be painless and quick. Even so, he found himself eschewing meat for a time.

Like a trick of magic, he began to recall the instructions he received. The first duty the creature gave him was to care for himself. He had allowed his hair to grow tangled and unkempt. His beard was long and matted, his clothes filthy. He had no razor and had to cut his beard off with a knife. Though he nicked his face many times, from the reflection in the water, he had to agree, that he looked much better clean and barefaced. When he was presentable, or as presentable as he was going to be, the creature returned briefly and told Greg to be watchful. Before Greg could ask more, the man-shaped creature with antlers like a stag vanished.

Greg took the boy's hand, the bones fragile in his large, calloused palm. He put a finger to his lips, cautioning the lad not to speak. Then he rushed toward the lights. His feet raced through the forest—he need not watch his step, only focus on his destination. The child became as light as a scarf. Greg drew him close to his side. Soon he saw the creatures the boy spoke of. They were wee, the size of Greg's hand, and flew with iridescent wings that glowed blue and beat so fast that they blurred. Little in the way of clothing graced their lithe bodies. Strips of lightweight material in shades of the forest—greens and browns—swathed their loins and the females' bosoms, but many wore feathers in their long hair. Dozens of them held the corners of a cape. On the cape, a young lassie lay. Her hair was a burnished bronze, the same as her brother's. Her ears stuck out a bit from her head, but she wasn't as noticeably jug-eared as her sibling, as his hair was much shorter. Four of the creatures stood on her shoulders, their faces close to her ears. Greg knew not what they said, but if he tried to listen too closely, his eyelids became heavy. They wove some sort of magic that kept the child still and quiet. The creatures paid him no mind, except to point and giggle at his braids. "Silly hair, we gave him silly hair," they prattled. *So, they underestimate me*, Greg thought. It should be easy enough to send these wee things back to where they belong.

Leaning against a tree watching was a boy with wise eyes the gray of slate that belied his youthful appearance. As he regarded Greg, Greg unwittingly slowed his pace. "Who are you?" Greg asked.

The pixies did not trouble the lad. "You ask for introductions at such a time, Greg Gillie, Keeper of the Forest?" The voice was high and light, yet ageless. He was a paradox of a being.

Greg gestured to the watchful pixies. "Is this your doing?"

"Nae, though I came to enjoy the chaos," he answered. After first tugging his leather vest down and brushing imaginary dirt off his patched, short pants the color of ochre, he walked toward them. "I have many names. One I am known by is Robin Goodfellow."

Greg had heard of this being. The stories portrayed him as mercurial and a knave, but he also radiated great power. "Please, Robin Goodfellow—" Greg couldna bring himself to use a less formal salutation. "— these bairns need help."

Robin Goodfellow's eyes narrowed. "Careful, Keeper. Requesting a favor of the fae may incur a cost much higher than you can afford. Though *you* have a task, a duty, you are still the interloper here."

The *thbalup* of hoofbeats filled the night air. When Greg heard a screaming, eldritch neigh, beads of cold sweat beaded on his forehead and fear sliced his heart. Greg lifted the frightened child in his arms. Iain buried his face in Greg's shoulder and quivered. Greg ken what the poor lad felt and wished he need not be exposed to that which approached. He was thankful the lass still slumbered, the pixies still singing at her ear, but they all cowered low and cast their eyes down. Greg set his shoulders. He didn't like the idea of Robin Goodfellow at his back, but he liked less the idea of what approached coming unseen.

The hunting party was almost upon them. Greg turned so the boy wouldna look up and see the fierce countenance he now faced. It was the one who chained him to this duty—the one who made him Keeper of the Forest. Like the pixies, Greg avoided looking this creature in the eyes. As his leviathan steed snorted, foam flicked from its curled lips. Its mad eyes, the ruby of a banked fire, rolled back in the horse's head.

The being's horned head turned and regarded Robin Goodfellow. "Do you interfere?" he asked, his voice harsh.

Robin Goodfellow buffed his nails on a corner of his vest, a put-upon sigh escaping his lips. "Never would I do such a thing. I merely come to witness."

"If you think I know not of your mischief, you are mistaken," the horseman growled.

"If *you* think you have any say over me, it shall not go well for you, O Horned One." The mis-en-scene was still and thick—menacing. Air squeezed from his lungs until Greg wheezed.

His chest tightened. An unpleasant, prickly feeling danced over his body.

"It does none good if we are at odds. Let us cease. This display frightens them," the horseman replied. And suddenly Greg was able to breathe freely. He and the lad gasped. "Well, Keeper of the Forest, creatures with ill intent have breached the boundary and threaten your kinfolk. What say ye?"

Somehow, though the interaction was terrifying, seeing Robin Goodfellow stand tall in the shadow of the Horned One lent Greg strength. He forced himself to meet the horseman's eyes. "I am ready and willing to do my duty as Keeper of the Forest."

Greg set the lad down so his hands would be free. "Iain, stay here, I'll fetch your sister." Greg snatched the child off the cape so fast that the ones holding it bounced high from the suddenness. He cradled the lass in his arms. The creatures—no, they were *pixies*, though how he ken the name, he had no clue—buzzed like angry bees. They dropped the cape and flew to him. Some circled his head until he became dizzy trying to watch. Sharp jabs stung his back and shoulders. The lass stirred and screamed when she saw the pixies and fought to get down. "Stop, Jilly. I am here to save you." She paused to look at him, taking in his snaky hair, and resumed screaming.

"Jilly's doll!" Iain shouted. He zigged around Greg and snatched up the toy, then pelted back to Greg. The pixies guarding the poppet shrieked and followed, quickly catching up to Iain. A dozen grasped the back of his shirt and tugged him off his feet. The boy fell backwards and the pixies scattered to avoid getting squashed.

Greg slid the shrieking girl to his hip and reached for the boy. He slung the child over his shoulder and ran. The pixies followed, tugging braids and jabbing him with miniature spears made from thorns tied to sticks. Greg forced himself to run faster. He reached the edge of the forest. A man with a lantern peered at him. "Iain? Jilly?" He scowled at Greg. "What are you doing with me bairns?" The man's eyes widened with fear when he saw what raced behind them.

Greg thrust the wee ones at their father. "Take your children and off with you," he gruffly bade them.

The man, smaller in stature than Greg, could only carry the girl. "Run, Iain. Run home to your mum," he urged his son. Iain dashed ahead.

The little girl stared over her father's shoulder. As Greg turned to face the pixies, he heard her piping voice. "Da, that man, he saved us from the fairies."

As the sound of the man and his children fleeing faded, Greg met the army. They swarmed him like vicious midges. He swept his hands at them but couldn't land a blow on the speedy fae. They darted in quicker than a blink and jabbed him until he felt like a pincushion. Most of the spears remained stuck in his body, but some that shallowly impaled him he brushed or shook off. He tried to take a step, but he couldn't move. He spared a moment to glance down. Pixies stood on the bridge of his feet weighing him down as others wove sticky spider's silk around his ankles. If he had only been tied down by a few, he could have pulled loose, but he had dozens of such encumbrances. They paused in their abuse to examine him. Three darted close and snagged the hem of his kilt. Greg batted at them with one hand and struggled to keep himself decent with the other. The pixies tittered. One flew toward his ear and, though he shook his head to avoid falling prey to their lullabies, their breath tickled him and the faint music he did hear made him blink sleepily. The buttons on his shirt popped off as the small nuisances sliced the threads. Wee hands worked on the belt that held his sporran.

"ENOUGH!" His voice changed and rang with power. It demanded obedience and respect. Somehow Greg had become something more. His hands glowed. Now when he swung at the pixies, they were flung back as easily as dandelions' seeds were blown off in a gentle breeze.

"Tis nae fair," He heard one complain. The rest took up his cry.

Cocky with his newfound ability, he made sport of them. "Tis fair, you wee, wicked midges. Back to where you came from or I will swat you like mosquitoes." He swung his hands at the nearest pixies and watched three tumble back into an elm. *Such power.* His chest swelled with pride and he grinned, then rearranged his expression to scowl, but not before the creatures had seen. Their wings fluttered faster and faster and their little hands squeezed into fists.

The largest pixie lit on a branch and regarded Greg. "He is indeed the Keeper of the Forest. We must remain in the woods, but you will rue making light of us."

The pixies gathered in a swarm and buzzed around him. Greg felt no more than a single, hard thrust on his back before their leader called out, "Let us flee to the Hill." Though they hurled insults, they didn't attack Greg again and soon the light of their wings vanished in the night.

"I suppose those are indeed what I am tasked with keeping away from the villagers. It would have been nice if he who gave me such duty told me how I was to do it." *Though a strapping man might have been taken down by those oversized dragonflies, I am too strong for them.* He shook his head and a brief chuckle escaped.

Greg sat on the forest floor and began to break the spider webs that held him one and two at a time. Once free, he ambled back to the place he had made a rustic bed in a hollowed-out oak. To his surprise, the tree had grown. The trunk was so large that it would have taken at least ten men holding hands to encircle it. He slid through the opening. Inside, a large knot of wood poked from the side like a ledge. The leaves and the blanket that he had used to make a bed were strewn on top and a pillow had been added. "Well now. This will save me building a lean-to when the weather grows cold." He would marvel over all that had happened later, but for now, he just wanted to sleep. He removed as many of the makeshift swords as he could and curled up on his new bed.

The next morning, Greg rolled from his bed and left his tree house. Outside, he reached his arms overhead, and stretched. Something hit his bum hard. He wheeled around. Robin Goodfellow stood behind him snickering.

"What was that about?" Greg asked the puckish knave.

Robin Goodfellow held his hands out before him, palms up, and smirked. "Just following directions." After sketching a mocking bow, Robin vanished. *What in the world?*

"Will I ever make sense of this place?" Greg muttered as he examined the front of his shirt. While the holes in his clothing were small, there were many and they would need to be repaired. The village grocer had the supplies he needed. There was no love lost between the owner, a McNeil, and him, but it had to be done. He wished he could find someone to help him with unplaiting his hair, but he wasn't going to expose himself to ridicule. "I should just cut it all off," he complained. By the time he finished, his stomach complained of hunger. His hair, while braid free, refused to lie down and sprung from his head. He grabbed the hobo bindle he had tied to a stick to transport things he foraged and set out.

Greg approached the counter in the shop. Mr. McNeil made him wait while he rearranged goods. Just when Greg was ready to reach across and smack the man, he asked, "How can I help you?"

"Last night, I saved the entire village from fae attack. I shouldna have to wait to be served. I need thread and a needle." Greg scanned the shelves. He hadn't had bread since he relocated to the woods. He knew the farmer's wife supplied the shop with baked goods and eggs. "And fetch me a loaf of bread."

McNeil gathered the items and set them in front of Greg. "That will be twenty pence."

When Greg left his cottage, he also left all his money. He had no idea what had happened to it. "I havena." As much as it pained him, he added, "Perhaps I could do some work to earn it. Chop wood or wash the shop windows."

"If you dinna have money then you'll not be getting your goods."

Greg bristled. He was Keeper of the Forest. How dare Mr. McNeil treat him so. "I offered compensation. I wouldna have need for these if you and the others would stay out of the forest." Mr. McNeil gathered the supplies, then paused. His mouth curved into a faint smile. "On second thought, there is a small task you could do for me."

"What?"

"I have an important letter that must be delivered, but I'm unable to leave the shop unattended. If you were to deliver it, I would let you have the supplies free of cost."

Greg didn't know why Mr. McNeil suddenly felt generous, especially to him, but quickly said, "I can do that."

Mr. McNeil went through a door in the back and returned with an envelope. "Do you know of the Oggs?" Greg nodded. "Mr. Ogg is a miner and he and his family live near the caves on the other side of the island. I would consider your bill paid in full if you delivered this to him."

It would be a long walk and Greg could hear the patter of raindrops, but he needed the supplies. "Aye, I can deliver it."

Mr. McNeil snorted as he handed Greg the envelope. Greg guessed he was amused that Greg was in debt to him. Greg tucked the paper inside his shirt and untied his bag so he could use the material as a crude cape. The needle and thread he stored inside his sporran. The bread, he could eat on the way.

Mr. McNeil followed Greg to the door and held it open. Before Greg cleared the threshold, Mr. McNeil released the handle and the door smacked Greg on the rear. He swung round to glare, but Mr. McNeil had already turned away, a loud guffaw ringing out.

At least his hair was lying flat. Wet, but not fuzzy like a caterpillar. He'd quickly left the village proper and the buildings that gave some shelter from the downpour. At first, he splashed through the puddles and clay, but then he thought to climb on top of the stone walls lining the road. The oiled cloth of his makeshift cape kept him dry from his shoulders down to his thighs, but every few minutes he had to wipe the water from his eyes and slick back his hair. He thought about trying to cut through the forest, but he wasn't sure if he could reach the Oggs from the rocky tor that abutted the forest in that direction. He estimated he was almost there when one of the stones shifted. He pinwheeled his arms and for a moment, he thought he could manage to stay atop, but the noise flushed out a capercaillie. When the hen burst from the undergrowth and squawked, Greg lost his fight with gravity and tumbled off the wall. The ground was boggy and soft, so only his dignity was hurt and thankfully no one witnessed it. He sat up and checked for the letter. It had slipped a bit so he repositioned it. As he did, a large male capercaillie clicked and called as it strutted out, tail feathers spread. Spring was mating time and he must have interrupted a courting. "Sorry, laddie. I am sure she will return shortly," Greg said. The bird's clicks deepened in pitch and the bird tipped back its yellow curved beak. Its beady eyes below the slash of red feathers regarded him. Greg stood and paused to catch his breath. Before he could hop on top of the wall once more, the capercaillie ran at him. "Back, you," Greg called out, waving his arms. The bird took flight and when Greg was below him, SPLAT! Dark berry-stained bird poop dropped on Greg's nose. He hastily wiped it off and then cleaned his hands as best he could on the mossy wall.

"If you were trying to catch your dinner, you're going about it the wrong way." A very pale man stood before him. "And this is my property, sir."

"I wasna hunting. Well, I wasna hunting birds. Besides, I am Keeper of the Forest. I have free range of the island. Are you Mr. Ogg?"

The rain had fled along with the birds. "Aye, I am and what would you be having need of me for?"

Greg slipped the envelope from his shirt and handed it to Mr. Ogg, who opened it. As he read, Greg advised, "And you keep yourself and your kin away from the woods."

Mr. Ogg finished, then shook his head and rubbed his chin. He looked at Greg. "Well, then. I canna help the grocer. However, I ken someone that might. You'll need to take this note to Mr. Samms. He has a farm just down the road."

"What does the grocer need?"

"Well, it's a private matter and none of your concern. You just go on now and deliver this to someone who can help." Mr. Ogg thrust the note into Greg's hand and turned to leave. As Greg left, he noticed Mr. Ogg's shoulders shaking.

The Samms Farm was in the opposite direction, but at least the walk would be rain free. But what in the world did the grocer do to require help? And what kind of help did he need that he thought a miner could aid him, but the miner believed a farmer should be consulted? A person as important to the village as he was should not have to run about with a note, he thought.

Greg decided to take a shortcut through the woods to reach the farm. Calling upon the gifts given to him, he sped through the forest and was at the back of the Samms property in minutes. "I hope Mr. Samms can take care of this. I want a bath and dinner," Greg mumbled. Greg knew Mr. Samms better than Mr. Ogg. The Oggs tended to keep to themselves, but before Greg lost his wife and child, they often saw the Samms family in the village.

Greg walked to the house and knocked on the door. When there was no answer, he knocked again. The farm was quiet. Had something happened to the family? Greg had expected to see Mr. Samms and his boys out working the fields. He knocked once more. When there was no answer, he cracked the door open. The fire was well stoked and two drying racks with clothes draped upon them sat before it along with a large wash tub full of sudsy water. Greg wandered closer to the fire. Perhaps he could dry his clothes before leaving for home. "Mrs. Samms, it's Greg Gillie," Greg called out.

The tub water churned and out popped the head of a young lass. She took one look at Greg and screamed. Greg stumbled back and ran into the clothing rack. Mr. Samms burst through the front door.

"What's going on?" He glared at Greg. "What are you doing in my home and why do you have my wife's corset?"

When Greg bumped into the rack, his belt got caught up on the laces of Mrs. Ogg's corset. He grabbed the offending item, then tossed it back onto the rack. "Nobody answered the door. I thought—"

"Get out! Get out, get out, get out!" the girl in the tub screamed.

"You heard the lass," Mr. Samms said. Greg raced for the door and when he opened it, a boot to his seat accelerated his exit.

Mr. Samms followed and shut the door behind him. "There'll be hell to pay tonight, I warrant," he said. "What's wrong with you?"

"I didna see anyone. I didna know she was in there—bathing. I never would have—"

"My oldest daughter may never speak to me again and my wife—I was supposed to be working in yon vegetable garden, but one of the horses got loose and I went with my lad to catch it. I never dreamed someone would come calling. Why are you here? We've seen naught of you since your—"

"Aye, well—Mr. McNeil asked that I take this note to Mr. Ogg, but Mr. Ogg believes it was meant for you."

Greg handed Mr. Samms the letter. He opened it, read it and made a choking sound that turned into a cough. "Well, now. I think this needs to go to someone of authority, Greg."

"I do not suppose you could deliver it."

"I've my womenfolk and farm to tend to. You need only go to the village and take the note to the constable."

"Aye, well then, I best be leaving. Thank you, Mr. Samms and I am sorry."

"So you say. Off with you before you cause any more trouble."

Greg ran through the forest. He wasn't sure where the constable's office was, but the tea shop lady directed him. He beat hard on the door. There was no way he was opening it.

An elderly man answered. "What? Are you trying to knock my bloody door down? Why dinna just come in?"

"I saw a naked girl last time I did that."

The man shook his head. "What are you on about, laddie?"

"Never mind. Mr. McNeil asked me to deliver this note to Mr. Ogg, but Mr. Ogg told me it needed to go to Mr. Samms and he told me I should take it to you."

"Give me the note." Greg handed him the note. He opened it and read it then burst out laughing. "Oh laddie, they tricked you fine."

"What do you mean?"

"Do you not pay attention to the date? Here, read." He handed the note to Greg.

It said, *Dinna laugh, dinna smile. Hunt the gowk another mile.* "You might also want to check your back," the constable said.

Greg reached over his shoulder and was just able to snag something attached to the back of his shirt. He ripped it free. It was a paper with the words "*KICK ME HARD FOR I AM SOFT*" printed upon it. "That explains why I've gotten several boots to the seat today." Greg thought back to the night before and the last jab in the back he received from the pixies. They were right, he did rue his treatment of them. "It's April first?"

"Aye, Huntigowk Day and you are the gowk, the cuckoo, the fool. Sorry lad, but you've been set off on a merry goose chase. I've ended it, though. Wouldna happened if you hadna been so high-handed all day. Word travels fast here, especially when those with news need not walk, but can ride instead. We ken your task, but just because you've been gifted skills to perform it doesn't make you better than the rest of us."

Greg ken the truth in this and shame bowed his head. He folded both papers and tucked them in his shirt. "Aye, and I will be keeping these to remind me." For so long, mourning had been the only thing in his life. Now, he had a purpose. But purpose or no, he was only a man at the heart of it all. Who knew when these powers faded? Had Robin Goodfellow granted him a boon by allowing the day to play out as it did? Better to be a laughingstock than a lifelong fool.

He strode toward the forest and his home, chuckling to himself and wondering about his next challenge.

The End

Don't miss out!

Visit the website below and you can sign up to receive emails whenever Zoe Tasia publishes a new book. There's no charge and no obligation.

https://books2read.com/r/B-A-MCFH-UCRCC

BOOKS 2 READ

Connecting independent readers to independent writers.

Did you love *A Happy Christmas Ceilidh*? Then you should read *Kilts and Catnip* by Zoe Tasia!

Danger lurks in the forest.

But Greg Gillie, a handsome Scot with a mysterious past, protects the Shrouded Isle and the lands beyond from the menacing fae.

A woman's arrival disturbs the Wee Folk.

Becca Shaw, an American widow, takes a family vacation to the island. Each day she remains, Greg struggles as more and more fae steal away from the forest hill and threaten the people.

Can the exodus be stopped?

As the danger increases, Becca strives to repair her relationship with her still-grieving girls and befriend the suspicious villagers. Resisting their blossoming feelings for one another, Greg and Becca team up to find answers. Why are the fae escaping? How can Greg and Becca stop them?

For their sake and the sake of the world, let's hope they're up to the task.

Kilts and Catnip, the first book in a new fantasy series, is filled with sweet romance, delightful humor, and exciting adventure.

"The settings are well-drawn, especially the author's descriptions of the tree-lined streets ("Roses twined up trellises along the walls, splashing yellows, pinks, and reds. Sun shone down on the leaves of the honeysuckle-garlanded oaks dappling the bright sidewalks with shade"). This promising new fantasy series with strong characters should appeal to fans of Charlaine Harris." Kirkus Reviews"By building a powerful atmosphere of family ties and then introducing a romantic and mysterious figure into the mix, Zoe Tasia has created an original, gripping story that draws readers in with not just evolving romance and fantasy, but strong interpersonal ties which lie at the heart of any truly compelling read. Kilts and Catnip is highly recommended for paranormal and romance audiences who want their writing vivid, personal, and as strong in psychological connections as it is in a sense of place and an atmosphere of danger; all set against a search for connections and home." D. Donovan, Senior Reviewer, Midwest Book Review

Read more at zoetasia.com.

Also by Zoe Tasia

The Shrouded Isle
Kilts and Catnip
Bagpipes and Basil
A Happy Christmas Ceilidh

Watch for more at zoetasia.com.

About the Author

Zoe Tasia grew up in Oklahoma and spent seven years in Scotland. Now she resides in the great state of Texas, where everything's bigger and better, or so she's told by the natives. Zoe is married to an understanding Greek, has two grown sons, and three cat overlords. When she's not giving her make-believe friends full rein, she enjoys the opera, ballet, well-chilled champagne and books. Bagpipes and Basil is the second book in The Shrouded Isle fantasy series. Kilts and Catnip, a finalist for the 2019 National Readers' Choice Awards and semi-finalist for the 2019 Ozma Book Awards, is the first book in her fantasy series, The Shrouded Isle. Three of her shorter pieces are published in the anthology, Quick Draw!: Fast and Funny Fiction. Zoe Tasia has also co-written three books published under the pen name Zari Reede.

Read more at zoetasia.com.